CIRCLE SIX PUBLISHING
PRESENTS

CORPORATE THUG

By: Marlin Ousley

Marlin Ousley

ISBN-13: 978-1727773262
ISBN-10:1727773268

Book Productions: Crystell Publications
You're The Publisher, We're Your Legs
We Help You Self Publish Your Book
E-mail – cleva@crystalstell.com
E-Mail – minkassitant@yahoo.com
www.crystellpublications.com
(405) 414-3991

Printed in the USA

Acknowledgements

With every book, acknowledgements become harder because I'm afraid that I'll leave someone out. So if for some reason you do not see your name, please forgive me.

God is still and forever will be number one because without his blessing none of this would be possible.

To my parents, thanks for instilling in me a never-quit attitude. I'm sure it's not easy accepting that your son writes street lit, but your support for me never wavered. I appreciated it and both of you.

To my kids, I love you all. The joy y'all bring to my life can never be measured. To my son Anthony, never forget that I'm your best friend and your greatest supporter. To my son Lil Marlin, I'm proud to call you mine. To my daughter Alexandria, the love I have for you inspires me to continue no matter how hard it gets.

To my family, Marlina, Audrey, Marvel, Tiara, Trellanie, Bobo (R.I.P.), Maya, Haps, J-Bo, D.J., Lil Willis, Mark, Marleane, Marvin, David, Karen, Bob, Gene, Aunt Cecile, Emani, Lil Marlin III, Maraya, Mizani, Anaya, Antonae, Nathan, Tara, Rocko, Noah, Misline, Cameron, Clarissa, Pooh, Anthony (R.I.P.), Taylor, and all those I'm close to, thanks for the love and support.

To my friends and supporters, Charlie Boy (no matter what, we still fam), Yancey, Terrence Green, Trese, Poochie, Red Rick, Kasha, Bam, James, Shawny, Shell (my #1 fan), Black Rick, and everybody else in the Bajas. Tamela (Daytona),

Bridgette (Pensacola), Roscoe (St. Pete), Toni (Kentucky), Terrio, Joe (Brown Sub), Pop Loso (Robin Hood), Gene (Jacksonville), Freddy Wilson (Ft. Pierce) and all the niggas and niggettes on lockdown, y'all keep y'all head ups.

To Crystal Perkins of Crystell Publication for all your help and insight. I thank you for putting up with my countless letters and inquiries, you are truly a blessing.

To those people who befriended me then tried to stab me in the back, I ain't mad at you 'cause you can't knock the hustle.

Thanks for all the people who spread the word about my books. Thanks to the thousands of people that wish me well and tell me to keep my head up. When I get home I'm throwing a big ass part and everyone's invited (LOL).

To my fans, for your continued support.

If I've forgotten anyone, don't take it personal. Either I've honestly forgotten or I don't fuck with you at all.

To those who told me I couldn't do it, do you believe me now?

To Ousley's everywhere, I'm about to take our game global so get ready for the ride.

Now sit back, relax, and enjoy, 'cause this shit's so real you'll think you lived it

Corporate Thug Part 1

Chapter 1

Brad Wesley, age forty one, sat in his downtown Miami office overlooking Brickell Avenue as he thought about his future. He'd graduated from the University of Miami's school of business at the top of his class and after interning at the brokerage firm of Cotton and Williams, he was given a job. Five years later, he was a top executive, having risen through the ranks using a take-no-prisoner approach. With his beautiful girlfriend Carla and his penthouse apartment on South Beach, he had everything a man could ask for.

Ten years earlier, he was known on the streets as Hood, a mean, vicious killer who controlled the drug trade and took no excuses. What started out as a simple means for him to pay for college turned into something much bigger and looking around his spacious office, he wondered if he could ever leave it all behind.

"Excuse me, Mr. Wesley," his secretary said while poking her head in the door.

"Yes, Ms. Patterson." He replied suddenly brought out of his reverie by the sound of her voice.

"Your one o'clock appointment is here to see you."

"Is it Mr. Tinaka from the Trans Corporation?"

"Yes it is, sir."

"Well could you please escort him to the conference room? I'll be there shortly."

"No problem, and shall I offer him some refreshments?"

"Yes, that'll be fine," Wesley replied. "Oh, and Ms. Patterson."

"Yes, Mr. Wesley?"

"Thank you."

Gathering his files, he stood as he prepared to meet Mr. Tinaka and with one last glance around the office, he headed for the conference room. As he entered, Mr. Tinaka stood to greet him.

"Mr. Wesley, it's good to see you."

"Likewise, Mr. Tinaka. And how have you been?" Wesley replied as the men shook hands.

"I'm fine, but you know how it is."

"Yeah, tell me about it. Please have a seat. Mr. Tinaka, I called this meeting because after going over your proposals, there are a few things I'd like to discuss with you."

"Oh!" Mr. Tinaka replied in surprise. "Is there something wrong?"

"No, not at all. I mean, nothing that can't be worked out."

"Ok, what is it that you would like to discuss?"

"Well, according to the proposals you submitted, your projected investment may not be enough for us to go ahead with the hotel project."

"Not enough! Mr. Wesley, I don't understand."

"Well, as you know Mr. Tinaka, we're in a recession right now. And due to the economic conditions, construction costs have soared. And then there are other risk factors involved."

"I can understand the construction costs rising because of the economy, but what are these risk factors you mentioned?"

"For one, we run the risk of losing our financing should our primary lender file for bankruptcy. But for an additional million dollars, we can move forward with the project and you'll receive an additional two percent share."

"That is ridiculous!" Mr. Tinaka replied, "We've been negotiating this deal for three years. But as you now sit here saying something else, I'm at a loss."

"Calm down, Mr. Tinaka. Yes, we've been negotiating this deal for some time. But as you well know, over the past year and a half the economy has been in a downturn and many sectors have taken a big hit—namely the real estate market. As it stands right now, with your investment including shares, you're looking to make an eighteen million dollar profit over five years. With an additional five million dollars, not to mention your added two percent in shares, you're looking to profit twenty two million dollars in the same amount of time."

"What happens if I refuse this new proposal of yours?"

"We'll return your initial investment and look for another investor."

"You can't do that!" Mr. Tinaka screamed as he stood, glaring at Wesley from across the conference table.

"I can and I will. Because, you see, we stand to lose a great deal of money if this project doesn't succeed."

"And if it does, you will gain considerably, will you not?"

"That is no concern of yours. In fact, you should be asking yourself if you want to lose twenty two million dollars because you chose to be stubborn."

"Being stubborn has nothing to do with it," Mr. Tinaka replied. "In fact, the point I'm trying to make is you and I agreed on one thing and now you're telling me something different, then on top of that, you give me an ultimatum."

"Well, I'm sorry if you look at it like that, but this is business and in business there's no room for personal feelings. I came to you with a deal that could net you twenty two million over five years because I thought you were a business man."

"And I am a business man."

"Yet you sit here and gripe about me hurting your feelings. I tell you what—the deal's off," Wesley said standing. "Your investment will be returned to you and, as I said, we will seek other investors."

"Wait a minute!" Mr. Tinaka shrieked. "Let's not get ahead of ourselves. There's no need for us to be at each other's throats. I mean, we're both business men, and the purpose of doing business is to make money, right?"

"Yes it is," Wesley replied. "But if you do not wish to do business with us, I'm sure we can find someone who will."

"Now, now, Mr. Wesley, I said nothing to indicate that I didn't want to do business with your company. I was merely trying to get an understanding of this new proposal."

"Well, can I take it that you will accept these new terms?"

"Most certainly," Mr. Tinaka answered with a hesitant smile. "And hopefully we can continue to do business in the future."

"Well that definitely won't be a problem," Wesley replied while gathering his files. "My secretary will fax you the paperwork no later than twelve this afternoon. Have your attorney go over it, sign the appropriate lines, and send us a notarized copy. Now you have a nice day, Mr. Tinaka. I have another meeting in ten minutes."

While escorting Mr. Tinaka out, Wesley winked at his secretary as they passed. After watching Mr. Tinaka leave, he headed for his boss's office. He entered without knocking and as his boss looked up, he threw the files on his desk.

"Well, did he go for it?" His boss asked.

"Hook, line, and sinker," Wesley replied, "and I made a little money in the process."

"You did what? How?"

"Well, the new proposal called for an additional four million in investments, with an added three percent share in the venture. I got him to agree to a five million dollar investment with an additional two percent share. The extra one percent goes to the company. Just have the million dollars transferred to my account."

"Damnit, Wesley!" His boss screamed. "You're gonna have to stop this."

"Stop what? For the last five years, I've made you over three million dollars and God knows how much for the company. Throw in the additional shares and it doubles, so don't get bent out of shape because I make a little on the side."

"Ok," his boss replied. "But you need to be careful 'cause if anybody finds out, we're both screwed."

"Don't worry about it, boss. I got it covered."

"Hmm, if you say so. Now, anything else?"

"Yeah, we have a meeting scheduled this Thursday with the Dana Corporation. I suggest we set it off and give them time to sweat."

"What if they decide to go somewhere else?"

"They won't, because no one's offering the kind of returns we are. Besides, I've sent someone to see one of them and make sure he doesn't change his mind."

"I don't even want to know," his boss replied. "Just make sure it doesn't backfire."

"Oh it won't, and when the deal's done, I'll throw in another two hundred thousand dollars. Maybe you can take your wife on a vacation or something."

"Yeah, that would be nice, wouldn't it?"

"Anyway, I'm gonna head on home," Wesley said, "My girl and I have a dinner engagement with a few community leaders to discuss donating some money to the new boys and girls club."

"Yeah, I heard about that."

"Gotta give 'em something to do besides run the streets, right?"

"Yeah, I guess you're right, but do you think building community centers will stop them from killing each other?"

"Who knows," Wesley replied. "But at least I'll give 'em a chance."

"Yeah, I guess so. Anyway, good job on the Tinaka deal. I don't know how you pull it off, Wesley, but you do."

"Yeah, well I'll see you in the morning." Wesley replied as he turned and headed for the door.

On the drive home, he pulled out his cell phone and dialed his girlfriend's number. As he waited for her to answer, he thought about how they'd met and how she'd react if she found out about his alternate lifestyle. She was from a well-to-do family and had grown up in Coral Cables, where drugs and violence were virtually non-existent. Now, after dating for almost four years, she still had no idea about his reputation in the streets and if he could help it, she never would.

"Hello!" He said suddenly hearing her voice.

"Oh, hi baby." She replied.

"I'm just calling to see how you're doing."

"I'm fine and I was just thinking about you. I'm at the mall trying to find something to wear to the dinner tonight. You do remember that we have a dinner engagement, right?"

"Yeah, I remember. You wouldn't let me forget..." He mumbled.

"Did you say something, sweetie? I didn't hear you."

"I just said I'm on my way home to get some rest."

"Ok, do you want me to pick out something for you to wear tonight?"

"Nah, I'm good. But I'll see you when you get home."

"Alright sweetie, I love you."

"I love you too," he replied before hanging up. And as he headed home, he suddenly realized he had something else to take care of and decided, *"Yeah, I'll take care of it now so tonight there will be no distractions."*

CHAPTER 2

After pulling up to a house in the Scott Lake Area, Wesley parked his car, got out, and opened his trunk. Once he retrieved his briefcase, he walked to the door and knocked, and several seconds later his friend Moose opened it.

"Damn nigga, what's up with the suit?"

"I just got off work," Wesley replied. "And I decided to stop by tonight because me and my girl got a dinner date with a few community leaders."

"Oh, you're still on that upstanding citizen shit, huh?"

"Call it what you want but it's the reason we've lasted as long as we have."

"You think so?"

"Hell yeah. I've been donating money to build youth centers and other projects around the neighborhood for how long now?"

"About four or five years."

"Yeah and not once has anyone questioned where the money comes from. And you know why?"

"Shit, they really don't care." Moose replied.

"Well, besides that—I've got a good job. And when you've got people like community leaders who look at you as an upstanding citizen, you can fly under the radar. The police have been trying to figure out who Hood is for the longest. With what I'm doing, do you think they'd even consider it was me?"

"Ok, you got a point. But you'll always be Hood to me."

"Yeah, but to them crackers, I'm Mr. Wesley. And I want to keep it like that."

"Alright, I feel you," Moose said, "But I ain't used to seeing you in no suit."

"Yeah, well don't get it twisted 'cause a nigga still Hood." Wesley replied.

"Alright, so what's up?" Moose asked while pointing to the briefcase.

"Just brought you some more shit. What you got left?"

"I got 'bout a half a key left. The money's in the room."

"Alright, well let me get that while I'm here and I'm gon' leave you with another six."

As Moose got up to retrieve the money, Wesley opened the briefcase and began removing the work. Moose returned to see the six more keys sitting on the table.

"Damn nigga, you ain't scared to be riding 'round with that shit?"

"Scared for what?"

"Shit—if the police pull you over and find that, ain't no way you gon' be able to explain that."

"First of all, I ain't got no warrants and my license, my registration, tag and insurance is up to date. If the police do pull me over, they would have no reason to want to search my car."

"Shit! A nigga driving a Jaguar is reason enough and you know that."

"Yeah, that might be true. But where niggas fuck up is when they buy these expensive cars and forget the details, like their license is suspended or somethin'. For instance, if the police pull you over and all your paperwork ain't up to date, you give them probable cause to search your shit. But if your shit's tight, then all they can do is write you a ticket for speeding or some other bullshit and send you on your way."

"Yeah, that sounds good and all, but I still won't be riding 'round with that shit in my car."

"Don't worry 'bout riding around with it." Wesley replied, "You just concentrate on getting rid of it."

"Yeah, I hear you."

"Now how much is that?" Wesley asked while pointing to the bag in Moose's hand.

"A hundred and ninety thousand, and I'll have another twenty once I get rid of the other half."

"Alright, keep the twenty for yourself and I'll holla back at you in a couple of days."

"Good looking out, nigga." Moose said smiling, "I mean, you always show love."

"Yeah, well you've always been straight with me. Besides, I don't trust too many people like I do you."

"I feel you."

"Good. Now I'm gon' head to the house to get a little sleep before this dinner tonight, so you be careful and call me if anything comes up."

"Alright, I got you," Moose replied as he watched his friend walk out to his car, get in and drive off. After walking back inside, he locked the door and got busy preparing the work for sale.

***

Across the street at Scott Park located on 178th Street and 17th Avenue, Spoon and his friend Germ watched as a shiny new Jaguar pulled off.

"Damn! I wonder who that was pushing that Jag?" Spoon screamed.

"I don't know," Germ replied. "But whoever it is, that nigga's paid."

"Yeah and we sittin' round here broke as a ma'fucka," Spoon said in disgust. "Man, don't you know U.M. supposed to be playing Florida State next month up in Tallahassee? We supposed to go up there stuntin'."

"And how the fuck we supposed to get up there?" Germ replied. "We ain't even got a car."

"That means we gotta get off our asses and go get it. Shit ain't just gon' come to a nigga sittin' round doin' nothin'. We gotta make it *happen.*"

"And how the fuck we gon' do that?"

"You ever hear of a nigga named Hood?"

"Hell yeah, I've been hearing 'bout that nigga since I was in elementary school."

"Yeah, well, that nigga done got old now and nobody don't respect him the way they used to."

"Man, what the fuck you talkin' bout? Them same niggas got Carol City on lock. Shit! Anybody who's getting work is getting it from them."

"Yeah, well all that's about to change."

"And how you figure that?"

"First of all, you see that house over there?" Spoon said while pointing to the house across the street.

"Yeah, what about it?"

"The old man who lives there probably works for that nigga Hood. And I bet you that whoever was driving that Jag does, too. He probably just dropped off some work."

"So what does that have to do with us gettin' money?"

"If we rob that old man... who knows what we might come up with."

"Nigga, is you crazy?!" Germ screamed. "What you tryin' to do, get us killed? When I was in high school, I heard a nigga ran off with some of his shit and when he caught him, he set him on fire then shot his ass."

"So what? You act like you're scared or something..."

"Nah, I ain't scared, it's just that..."

"Just what?"

"Man, them ma'fuckers got all kinds of ma'fuckers working for them. Ain't but two of us, how we gon' go up against them niggas?"

"First of all, them niggas is old, their time is gone. We young niggas and it's our time to get money. Shit, I can name fifteen to twenty young niggas right now who wanna get paid. We rob that nigga and whateva we get, we put young niggas on and we run shit how we want to run shit."

"Man, I don't know…" Germ said shaking his head. "Them niggas find out we got their shit, they gon' be ready to go to war."

"That just means we'll have to be ready for war, too," Spoon replied. "Look man, I'm tired of being broke and seeing everybody else getting' money. This is our opportunity to get paid. But if you don't want no money, that's cool. I'll just go find some niggas that do."

"Hold up!" Germ shot back. "We've been friends since elementary school and I've always had your back, but man, this is some other shit."

"What you mean, this some other shit?"

"I mean, we both know this nigga, or at least heard about him."

"So what?!"

"So, if we do this, we gotta be willing to go all out if it comes to that and so does anybody we bring in. Are you willing to do that?"

"Hell yeah!" Spoon replied, "Like I said, it's our time to get some money and right now, it's whateva."

"Alright, then I'm with you. But first, we gotta find some young niggas who want to get paid."

"Oh, that ain't gon' be no problem," Spoon replied. "And I know just where to look."

***

Back at Wesley's penthouse apartment, he was just getting out of the shower and as he began drying off he thought about tonight's dinner. He didn't really like rubbing elbows with all the politicians, but he figured it was better to have them on your side rather than against you. To him, politicians were evil. They'll say all the right things to get elected and once in office, they do nothing to help the community. They'd fight to get laws passed to seem tough on crime, yet they violate the very laws they propose. Sure, when something happens they'll hold rallies, give press releases and whatever else to score political points. But as soon as things die down, they go back to doing nothing.

He, on the other hand, knew what it was like to have nothing to do as a child. So even though he played both sides of the fence, he was compelled to do something to help the generation after him by providing money for neighborhood youth centers, sponsoring little league football teams, turkey and toy drives—anything and everything. He considered himself a man of the people. He made a six figure income at his job, brought in over two thousand a month, not including the money form his side hustle at work, and was looked upon as an upstanding citizen for his contributions. He smiled to himself as he climbed into bed, and as he closed his eyes, his last thought was *"Only in America."*

CHAPTER 3

"Nigga, y'all ma'fuckas gotta be crazy!" Clarence screamed. "Y'all know who Hood is?"

"Man, fuck that nigga. I'm talking about us getting *paid*."

"Yeah, I know what you're talkin' about." Clarence replied, "But what I want to know is how we gon' get paid if all of us are dead? That nigga Hood been killing ma'fuckers before we were born. What you think he gon' do if he finds out that not only did we take his shit but we're trying to take over, too?"

"You know what?" Spoon said angrily, "I'm tired of everybody talking about this nigga like he's the only ma'fucka who can kill someone. Y'all act like he can't die."

"Man, that nigga been out here for a long time and don't too many people know who he is."

"Look, all I'm trying to do is get paid, I don't care 'bout all that other shit."

"Yeah, but ain't no need for us to get killed for nothing," Clarence replied. "Now, you said that all you wanted to do was get paid, right?"

"Yeah, that's what I said."

"Well, I know a way we can get paid and we won't have to go through all that bullshit."

"Man, what the fuck you talking 'bout?" Spoon screamed.

"I'm talking 'bout you trying to rob the old man who works for Hood."

"How else we gon' get paid? He damn sure ain't gon' just give it to us."

"Nah, he definitely ain't gon' do that," Clarence said. "But you know if we rob him like you're talking 'bout, we gon' have to kill him."

"So what? I ain't got no problem with that."

"I didn't say you did, but why do that and bring heat on us when we can break in his shit and nobody will now who did it? By the time they find out that it was us, we'd have gotten rid of the shit and we'll have enough niggas down with us to deal with whatever."

"Now, that sounds like a plan!" Germ screamed. "I mean, at least this way we won't have to kill nobody—not yet, anyway."

"Alright!" Spoon replied, "But I'm telling you, if one of them ma'fuckas come round here with that bullshit, it's whateva, and I'm dead ass serious."

"Alright, check it," Clarence said. "Only the three of us know about this and that's how we gotta keep it. We'll chill on the park till we see the old man leave and when he does, one of us will watch out while the other two go in."

"That's straight," Spoon replied. "But shouldn't at least one of us have a gun just in case the old man comes back?"

"I can get a three fifty seven from my cousin." Clarence said.

"Ok, well go handle that and meet us back here. Meanwhile, we gon' watch and wait for the old man to leave. Hopefully, by the time you get back, he'll be gone, 'cause I'm ready to get this shit over with."

"Yeah, me too," Germ replied.

"Well, y'all chill and I'll be right back," Clarence said before walking off. While watching him leave, Germ turned to face Spoon.

"Man, I hope we know what we're doing."

"When we start getting this money, you won't be asking that," Spoon replied.

***

Back on South Beach, Wesley's girlfriend walked in to find him still sleep.

"Wesley!" She shrieked.

"Huh—what?" He replied waking up.

"Sweetie, it's four o'clock and we have to be at dinner by six!"

"Damn Carla, that's two hours from now, we've got plenty of time."

"Yeah, but you know how I like to get there early and we don't want to get caught in traffic."

Slowly rolling out of bed, Wesley stood and watched his girlfriend walk back and forth getting ready for tonight. Seeing her in her panties and bra aroused him and figuring he had time, he approached her from behind. Reaching around her, he cupped her breasts while pressing his hard-on against her behind.

"Wesley, what are you doing?" She grumbled while grabbing his hands.

"What do you mean, what I'm doing? I'm trying to make love to my woman."

"Not now, we have to get ready."

"The dinner's in two hours, we have more than enough time for a quickie."

"A quickie?" she replied while turning to face him. "Do I look like a cheap two dollar whore to you? You figure you can just get your rocks off for two minutes and that's ok? Well, a quickie doesn't do it for me. Besides, you might mess up my hair and I don't want to go to dinner smelling like sex."

"Mess up your hair?" Wesley said, clearly upset. "Here it is I want to have sex with my girl and all you can think about is your hair getting messed up?"

"Now, now," she said trying to calm him. "You know I love making love to you. It's just that I don't want to be late for the dinner engagement. What do you say we wait till after we get back, then I can make love to you all night?"

Without responding, he turned before going into the bathroom and closing the door.

As Carla continued getting dressed, she thought, *"That'll show him. If he thinks he's gonna use my body, he's in for a surprise. I want that ring on my finger and until then, I'll decided when and how my body is used."*

As Wesley stood under the water frustrated, he knew that he had to do something about her bourgeois attitude. Since they'd been together, she'd always been uptight when it came to sex, not allowing him to fuck her in certain positions, saying that was for whores. Oral was out of the question because in her mind, that was to be done only between husband and wife, and while he tried to respect her principles or whatever she called it, there were times when he wanted to have straight uninhibited sex. Well if she wanted to play these kinds of games, he'd show her that he could play them as well. While he portrayed the sophisticated businessman, what she didn't realize was that underneath that persona, he was still all Hood.

Climbing out of the shower, Wesley dried off and walked out of the bathroom still naked to find his girlfriend half dressed.

"Feeling better?" she asked. "I'll make it up to you tonight after we return from dinner."

"I got things to do after dinner," He replied.

"Things to do? What could be more important than making love to me?"

Receiving no reply, she walked over to him and reached out to caress his dick, but he grabbed her hand. Snatching it back, she looked up at him with contempt.

"Oh, so now you don't want me to touch you?"

"It's not that. I just don't want us to be late for our dinner."

"A minute ago you wanted a quickie and now you're concerned about being late?"

"Yeah, so let's get dressed so we can get out of here."

"Fine, if that's how you want it," She replied with an attitude. "You just remember that tonight when we get back."

"That'll be the last thing on my mind when we get back."

"And what's that supposed to mean?"

"It means shut up and get dressed so we can get out of here. Either that or I'm gonna leave you. It's your choice."

Knowing she had no win when he got like that, Carla finished getting dressed in silence. When they were ready to go, Wesley made sure everything was locked and while riding the elevator down, neither said a word. After reaching his car, they both climbed in and as he started it up and drove off, they both knew that tonight would be anything but boring.

CHAPTER 4

In the park, Spoon and Germ sat watching Moose's house waiting for him to leave.

"So you think he gon' get the gun?" Germ asked.

"I hope so," Spoon replied, "'cause we damn sure might need it."

Suddenly looking up, they spotted Clarence approaching smiling like the cat who ate the canary.

"Man, y'all ain't gon' believe this shit," he said.

"Ain't gon' believe what?" Germ asked.

"Remember I told y'all that I knew where I could get a three fifty seven?"

"Yeah, but man don't tell us you couldn't get it."

"Nah, I got it. But instead of one, I got two."

"Man, don't be bullshittin'."

"Do it look like I'm bullshittin'?" Clarence shot back while pulling up his shirt to reveal not one but two pistols.

"Oh shit! That nigga for real!" Germ screamed.

"Damn right I'm for real," Clarence replied as he handed one of the guns to Spoon. "The last time I found my cousin's stash spot, all he had in it was the .357. Today, I go back and he got the .357 and a .9mm. So I took 'em both."

"You sure he ain't gon' trip when he finds out his shit's gone?"

"He might, but if we break him off a little something, he'll be alright."

"Shit, if we get a nice enough lick, we could probably buy 'em from him," Germ said smiling.

"Yeah, all that sounds good, but we have to get in first."

"Well ain't that what we here for?"

"Yeah," Spoon replied while tucking the gun in his pants, "and we ain't going nowhere till that ma'fucka leaves."

***

Inside of Moose's house, he was cooking up the last of the work and thinking about the money that he was going to make. Him and Wesley's friendship went back twenty years and he remembered when neither of them had anything. Then, Wesley had the notion to go to college. But there was one problem: how was he gonna pay for it when he had no money? Together, they came up with a plan to make enough money to pay back Wesley's tuition. After Wesley finished college, he'd start his own business and hire Moose. Unfortunately, things didn't work out as planned. Instead, with their ruthlessness, they quickly became major players in the game and as the years passed, they had Carol City on lock.

A lot of dealers bought work from them and as Moose tended to the day-to-day operations, Wesley quickly became the astute businessman. His goal was to uplift the younger generation by providing them with opportunities that would break the cycle of despair, violence, and incarceration that many of them faced. Although they'd both made enough money to retire many times over, they figured what's the use? Moose was the face of the organization, the one everybody saw and dealt with, and Wesley was the one who kept everything running smoothly. But if things got out of hand, he became Hood, the gold-toothed Grim Reaper. Hardly anyone knew that Wesley was in fact Hood and he loved it that way, because in the eyes of the community he was an upstanding, no-frills businessman who dedicated his life to helping the younger generation. Well, that's what he wanted them to think, anyway.

As Moose waited for the work to dry, he busied himself cleaning the utensils and had to chuckle to himself. He'd just told Wesley about riding around with all the work in his car and here he was about to do the same thing. Finally finished with the cleaning, Moose packaged two keys for sale and stashed the other four and a half in his bedroom closet. After getting dressed, he locked up the house, went outside to his truck, and headed out. It was time to earn his money.

***

"There he goes," Spoon said as they all watched Moose get in his truck and drive off.

"Yeah, but let's chill for a minute, just in case he comes back." Clarence replied.

"Alright, but who's gonna go in with me?" Spoon asked.

"Shit, I'll go," Germ replied. "And Clarence can watch out to see if he comes back."

"Nigga, why can't I go and you watch out?" Clarence complained.

"'Cause we're the ones who came up with the idea in the first place."

"Yeah, but if it wasn't for me getting the guns…"

"Man, will y'all two shut the fuck up! Y'all sound like a bunch of bitches." Spoon said. "We all in this shit together so it makes no difference who goes with me and who watches out."

"Yeah, you're right." Clarence replied. "In that case, I'll watch out for the old man. But what I'm supposed to do if he comes back?"

"Honestly, I don't care, but if that ma'fucka comes back while we're in there, I'm gon' murk his ass."

"Man, let's just get this shit over with." Germ said, "That way, we can be in and out before he does."

"Alright, then let's go." Spoon replied.

As Clarence watched, both Spoon and Germ began walking across the park towards 17th Avenue. Once they reached the corner, they doubled back and began walking up the sidewalk toward the house. Being careful not to arouse suspicion, they reached the house, opened the front gate and walked to the door. Then after knocking several times and receiving no answer, they headed around to the back of the house.

"Man, how the fuck we supposed to get in?" Germ asked.

"Will you just shut up and make sure ain't nobody looking?" Spoon shot back. Then without another word, he pulled the pistol from his waist and kicked in the door. With the pistol out, Spoon rushed inside as Germ followed close behind. They found the house empty after a quick search. Suddenly turning to face Germ, Spoon said, "Alright, listen: I'm gon' search one room while you search the other. Make sure you look everywhere, under the bed, in the closet, dresser, shoe boxes—everything. That old man's got something in here, I just know it."

"I got you," Germ replied as he spun on his heels and headed for one of the rooms where he began flipping mattresses, pulling out dresser draws and removing everything from the closet. Meanwhile, in the other room, Spoon was doing the same.

Having searched two of the rooms and finding nothing, they both began searching the last one. It didn't take them long to find what they were looking for. Pulling a bag out of the closet, Spoon opened it up and found a scale and began frantically searching for what he knew was there.

"I got it!" he screamed while pulling out a duffel bag and opening it to reveal four and a half keys of cocaine wrapped in plastic.

"Damn! We done hit the ma'fuckin' jackpot."

"Yeah," Spoon replied smiling, "I told you it was here."

"You think there might be some more?"

"I don't know but let's see," Spoon said as they began ransacking the house. After finding about three thousand dollars in cash and another gun, he handed the gun to Germ. "Now we all got one."

After leaving out the way they came in, they walked calmly back towards the front of the house, out the front gate, and up the street.

Clarence smiled to himself when he saw them coming out of the house carrying the bag and wondered what they'd found. He didn't have to wonder long as Spoon and Germ walked up smiling.

"Man, we found almost five keys up in that bitch," Germ said.

"Damn, you serious?" Clarence asked.

"Hell yeah, and we found another gun."

"Look, we need to get out of the park with this shit 'cause when the old man gets back, he gon' come looking for whoever broke into his house," Spoon said.

"Man, fuck that old man," Germ replied angrily. "If he come round here, I got somethin' for his ass."

"A nigga get a gun and he gets all the heart in the world," Spoon said smiling. "Nigga, I'm talkin' 'bout going somewhere till we figure out what we gon' do next."

"Shit! We can go to my house," Clarence replied. "My ol' woman's at work and she don't get off till later."

"Alright, then come on," Spoon said. As they all headed to Clarence's house, all they could think about was money, clothes, and more.

CHAPTER 5

Arriving thirty minutes early, Wesley and Carla were greeted with warm smiles as they were escorted to their table. Still in a foul mood, Wesley remained silent as Carla made small talk with the other women seated at the table. Suddenly, he was approached by a man he didn't recognize and as he looked up at the stranger, the man spoke.

"Mr. Wesley, I'm the County Commissioner, Bob Mitchell, it's a pleasure to meet you. I've heard so much about your contributions to the city of Miami Dade County and I wanted to commend you for such fine work. It's not every day that such an accomplished businessman as yourself would take an interest in trying to help our youth."

"Well," Wesley replied while standing to shake the Commissioner's hand. "I'd have to say the pleasure's all mine. And as for trying to help the younger generation, well, I was young once. With a lot of the older black males strung out on drugs or in prison, the younger generation lacks guidance. So they seek it in the streets. Forming gangs gives them a sense of family and engaging in illegal activities not only provides them with the money they lack, but also the material possessions in which they define their self-worth. I'm trying to break that cycle by sponsoring youth programs and youth centers. I'm hoping to teach our younger generation the importance of education and that by acquiring knowledge, they'll have a better chance of succeeding."

"Mr. Wesley, we need a lot more men like you," Mr. Mitchell replied. "Because we're losing our young men to drugs, violence, and incarceration at an alarming rate. With the youth centers you sponsor, you're giving them an opportunity to learn life skills and hopefully many of them will take advantage of it."

"Mr. Commissioner, while providing youth centers is a start, much more is needed if we are to save this so called 'lost generation.' You see, we as black men must do more than pay lip service to the growing problems in our neighborhoods. We must begin to play an active role in the development of these kids and steer them in the right direction. We must go back to the old values when the community raised our children and made sure that all of them feel like they belonged."

"I totally agree with you," Mr. Mitchell replied. "But what sort of ideas do you have about starting such programs?"

"I'm glad you asked that," Wesley said with a smile. "Because that's the very thing I plan to address tonight and as County Commissioner, you can play a very important role."

"Good, and I look forward to hearing what you have to say. It's been a pleasure meeting you."

"Likewise, Mr. Mitchell. I look forward to working with you in the future."

"Who was that?" Carla asked as the Commissioner walked off and Wesley took his seat.

"That was Bob Mitchell, the County Commissioner."

"I didn't know you knew him."

"I didn't until a minute ago, but he seems like a nice fellow."

"What did he want?" Carla continued. Wesley became irritated by her questioning.

"That's not important."

"Look," Carla replied with a stern look, "I'm trying to be cordial, at least."

"Ladies and gentleman," the announcer suddenly said cutting her off. "May I have your attention, please. I'm Miami Dade County Commissioner Bob Mitchell and I appreciate you all taking time out of your busy schedule to be here tonight for this wonderful occasion. As you well know, we have a growing dilemma in our community that needs to be addressed. Our kids are running rampant and killing each other at an alarming rate. Teen pregnancy is at an all-time high, and AIDs has become the number one killer of African Americans between the ages of nineteen to forty four. If we don't do something now, it will have a lasting effect on our people for generations to come."

"How can we do something about the younger generation when they're so disrespectful to authority?" someone shouted.

"We have to make them listen," Mr. Mitchell replied. "Or we're gonna continue losing them to the streets or the many prisons being built across the nation. Tonight, we have someone in attendance that I'd like to introduce you to. This young man has set an example of what it's going to take for us to win our children back and break the cycle of destruction. His sponsorship of youth centers and intramural sports programs have given some of these children hope for a better future. We must continue to build on that if we are to save them. Ladies and gentlemen, I proudly introduce to you Brad Wesley, please welcome him on stage."

The room erupted in applause as Wesley stood and made his way to the podium. Dressed in an all-black Armani suit, he made a striking figure and many of the women in attendance took notice. Reaching the podium, Wesley looked out into the crowd, then raising his hand to quiet them, he began.

"Ladies and gentlemen, I'd like to thank the commissioner for this opportunity as well as you all for coming out tonight. We have a problem with our younger generation and we simply cannot ignore it any longer. We as the elders in our community must take a stand or risk losing a whole generation of young people. Growing up right here in Miami Dade County, I attended public schools and was raised in section eight housing by a single mother who never gave up on me. We cannot give up on our youth because to do so would mean that we have failed. Ladies and gentlemen, I stand before you tonight and I say to you that failure is not an option."

"That's right, brother!" someone else screamed.

"We've got our first black president and they said it would never happen. They say that there's no hope for our children, that they're too far gone and I say to you tonight that they're wrong on all accounts. Instead of just focusing on becoming a famous basketball player, football player, rapper or drug dealer, they should be aspiring to become doctors, lawyers, judges and, yes, even President of the United States."

The room erupted in applause as people stood to cheer him on and as Carla sat in amazement at their reaction to his words, all she could think about was becoming Mrs. Carla Wesley. Finally quieting down, everyone took their seats as he continued.

"Each and every one of us in this room got to where we are because someone believed in us, because someone wouldn't let us quit, because someone didn't give up on us. And ladies and gentlemen, I believe in our younger generation. I believe that they're worth saving and I will not give up on them. Tonight, I pledge fifty thousand dollars towards the Northwest Girls and Boys Club which will include a Cultural Arts Center, a state-of-the-art computer lab, and a theatre for the Performing Arts Center. I urge you to contribute because as our forefathers once said, it takes a community to raise a child. Thank you."

Again, the room erupted in applause as people stood to congratulate him. As Wesley made his way back to his seat, he was greeted with hugs, handshakes, and a few indecent proposals from women he'd just met. One such woman was Assistant States Attorney Eyvette Summers, who vowed to have him at all costs.

Finally seated back at the table, Wesley sat stunned when Carla announced, "Ladies, this is Mr. Wesley, my fiancé, isn't he wonderful?"

"He most certainly is," one lady replied.

"And handsome, too," said another.

"Ah, did I interrupt something?" Wesley asked while looking around the table curiously.

"No sweetie, I was just telling these lovely ladies how special you are."

"So what's this about you being my fiancé?"

"Oh that, well we were just talking and I explained to them that we were in the process of getting engaged."

"Oh really?" Wesley replied. "Well I wish you would've discussed it with me first before you go around spreading rumors."

"I just thought—"

"Well you thought wrong." Wesley shot back. Her face turned red from embarrassment.

"So," a young lady said, "being that you're not engaged, Mr. Wesley, would it be safe to say that you're single at the moment?"

"Well, Ms… I'm not sure what you name is, but I'm certain you didn't come here to inquire about my relationship status. Besides, Carla is my date tonight and it would be inappropriate to discuss this further. Now if you'll please excuse me, I'd like to enjoy my dinner."

"As you wish, Mr. Wesley," the woman replied with a smile. "As you wish."

The rest of the evening went fairly well as he occasionally made eye contact with Ms. Summers from across the room. Carla remained silent, which was alright with him, and he got the opportunity to meet some very influential people. As the night wound down, Wesley found himself wondering about Ms. Summers and decided he'd pursue the matter at a later time. Carla was still his date and due that respect. After saying their goodbyes, he and Carla left the building, climbed into his car and headed home.

"I can't believe you embarrassed me like that in front of all those people," Carla shrieked as soon as they were out of the parking lot.

"Well if you had talked to me first, you wouldn't have had to worry about being embarrassed."

"Couldn't you just have agreed with me and left it at that?"

"No, because then I would have been agreeing to something that wasn't true."

"So do you even plan on proposing to me?"

"Do you really want me to answer that?" Wesley replied while looking directly at her.

"Yes, I do. I asked, didn't I?"

"Alright then. No."

"No! So all this time I've been waiting for you to propose was for nothing?"

"See that's your problem, you think everything's about you and what you want. Ever since we've been in this relationship, not once have you ever asked what I wanted. We only have sex when you want to and even then it's 'Wesley, I don't do that' or 'Wesley, I want to do it like this.' Damn Carla, I have needs too, have you ever thought about that?"

"Oh, so that's what this is about?"

"No, it's about you acting like a stuck up bitch. And I'm tired of it. I try to respect you and your wishes, but it's never enough for you so I figure why keep trying."

"Well I never knew you felt like this," Carla replied.

"That's just it, if you took the time to focus on other things besides yourself, you'd know, but I don't think you're capable of that. Do you realize how many times I've wanted to go out and find another woman to sleep with, but I didn't because I wanted to respect your feelings? Carla, look, I love you. If I didn't, I'd have gotten rid of you a long time ago. But you need to stop being so uptight all the time and learn to live a little. I mean, I enjoy making love to you but sometimes, I just want to throw you down and fuck the shit out of you."

"In other words, treat me like a whore?"

"No, not like a whore, like my woman, but you know, try different things."

"Ok, well what if I tell you I'm willing to try?" she said while turning to face him.

"That's a start, but what happens after that?"

"We'll just have to see, won't we? Now here are the terms."

"No terms, it's either my way or no way."

"That's not fair and you know it."

"Life isn't fair, and up until now I think I've been more than fair with you and it hasn't gotten me nowhere."

"So you've decided to play hardball, is that it?"

"That's right," Wesley replied sternly.

"Ok. What do I have to do?"

"You'll find out when we get home."

CHAPTER 6

"Man, we gon' get paid for real," Germ hollered as the three of them stood in Clarence's room looking at the four and a half keys of coke laid out on his bed.

"Yeah," Clarence replied, "but first, we gotta find somewhere to get rid of it."

"Shit, what about the Carol City apartments?" Spoon asked suddenly.

"Ain't that where that nigga Todd was putting in work?"

"Yeah, but the Feds got him."

"It wouldn't have mattered if he was still out," Spoon said, "'cause now we got work and we got guns so as far as I'm concerned, it's whatever with whoeva. Like I told y'all earlier, I'm trying to get paid and I ain't trying to hear all that other shit."

"Oh a nigga feelin' that, but what we gon' do 'bout cooking this shit?" Germ asked.

"My cousin knows how to do that." Clarence replied.

"You think you could holla at him?"

"Yeah."

"Well handle that and tell him we'll break him off decent. Don't tell him how much we got. When that old man finds out his shit's gone, he gon' be looking for a ma'fucka with a lot of dope. If your cousin asks, just tell him all we got is a quarter key. It ain't his business where we got it from."

"Yeah, the less anybody knows the better."

"Right. Now Germ, I want you to go to the flea market and get us a digital scale so we can weigh this shit and some bags."

"Ok, but what I'm supposed to buy it with? 'Cause I ain't got no money."

"Oh yeah!" Spoon replied, while digging in his pocket. "I found about three thousand dollars in the old man's crib, so that's about a grand for each of us."

As he began passing out the money, Germ and Clarence looked on excitedly.

"I'm gon' keep a hundred dollars from everybody so we can buy all the shit we need to get this shit ready, and when it's time to pay Clarence's cousin for cooking the shit, we'll do it the same way."

"Alright, that's cool," both Germ and Clarence replied.

"But who you know in the Carol City Apartments for you to be talking 'bout going over there opening up shop?" Clarence asked.

"This girl name Sonya, who I used to kick it with. Why?"

"Nah, I'm just asking."

"Alright, then check it," Spoon said turning serious. "If we gon' do this, we all in, you feel me? Now I'm gon' holla at this broad Sonya to see what's up, but if she ain't wit it then it's still on."

"Nigga, you know we gon' be down with you no matter what," Germ replied. "We just don't want to be in the blind."

"Well, now y'all know what time it is, so Clarence call your cousin and ask him about cooking this shit for us."

"Alright, I got that."

"Germ, you go to the flea market and get the stuff we need so we can get this thing poppin'. In the meantime, I'm gon' swing by the apartments and holla at Sonya. Everybody meet back here, and we'll go from there."

"Alright," Germ replied as he got ready to leave. And as Clarence picked up the phone to call his cousin, Spoon left to go talk to Sonya.

***

After parking his truck in the driveway, Moose got out and noticed his next door neighbor outside watering her grass. "Hi, Ms. Marshall," he said while waving and all he could do was chuckle to himself as she waved back.

Ms. Marshall was seventy five years old and had retired years ago. Now living on retirement benefits, she spent most of her days either inside her house or tending to her yard, and she saw everything.

Putting down her water hose she called out, "Hey young man," and Moose turned in the direction of her voice. "While you were gone, two guys were looking for you."

"Yeah?" he replied with a puzzled look, "Did you see what kind of car they were driving?"

"They didn't have one, at least not one I saw."

"So how did they get here?"

"They walked from down there." She said while pointing down the street.

"What did they look like?"

"Like two little punks if you ask me. You know, the ones who always look like they're up to no good."

"So what did they do when they came looking for me?"

"They knocked on the door but when you didn't answer, I saw them go around to the back of the house."

"To the back of the house?"

"To the back of your house, but I couldn't see what they were doing. I was gonna call the police but you know how I don't like them so I waited for you to get back."

"Thanks, Ms. Marshall. Did you see them when they left?"

"Yeah, and one of them was carrying a bag or something. I couldn't tell you what was in it, my eyes ain't what they used to be, you know."

"I understand," Moose replied, "but did you see which way they went when they left?"

"Yeah, back the way they came."

"Ok, Ms. Marshall, thank you for looking after my place, but I need to go inside to check to see if everything is ok."

"Alright," Ms. Marshall replied, "but these kids nowadays ain't got no respect for other people's stuff. That's why I be keeping my eyes on them."

"Ok, Ms. Marshall, thanks again," Moose said as he began walking toward his door and with his heart pounding in his chest, he pulled out his keys and slid it in the lock.

After unlocking the door, he pushed it opened and stepped inside and instantly his worst fears were realized—someone had broken into his house.

***

Sonya was braiding her daughter's hair when she heard a knock at the door. Getting up to answer it, she opened it to find Spoon standing on her doorstep.

"What you want with your broke ass?"

"Girl, go on with the bullshit," Spoon replied, "I came 'round here to holla at you 'bout something."

"About what, Spoon? 'Cause I ain't got time for your games. I fell for that shit one time, I ain't falling for it no more."

"Damn! You gon' let a nigga in or what?"

"Why you can't say what you gotta say right here?"

"Look, I came to talk to you about something important. Give me five minutes and if you don't like what I'm saying, I'll leave."

After thinking about it for a second, Sonya agreed. "Five minutes, that's it."

After letting him in and closing the door, she turned to her daughter. "Tiffany, go to your room," and as her daughter stood and walked off, she turned to face Spoon with her hand on her hip.

"Alright, listen," Spoon said, "you know that nigga Todd in jail?"

"What that got to do with me?"

"I'm thinking 'bout opening up shop 'round here."

"Nigga, please!" Sonya replied laughing. "First of all, you ain't got no money. And second, who gon' give you some dope?"

"Shit done changed since the last time you saw me, but that's not important. What is, is the fact that I'll give you five hundred dollars a month to start if you'll let me stash my shit here."

"Nigga, if you give me five hundred dollars a month, you can stash whatever you want in here and I might even give you some pussy every now and then."

"Oh yeah?" Spoon replied before reaching in his pocket to pull out a wad of cash. "Well I tell you what, here's two fifty so you know I ain't bullshittin', and you'll get the other two fifty when I open up."

"Damn! Who the fuck you done robbed?"

"Why a nigga gotta done robbed somebody?"

"'Cause when you was fuckin' with me, you ain't never had no pocket full of money."

"Yeah, well like I said, shit done changed since the last time you saw me."

"Oh, I can see that," Sonya replied with a smile. "You walking around with your pockets all on swole and talking about opening up shop, hell yeah, shit's done changed."

"Anyway, we got a deal, right?"

"Hell yeah! Just have my other two hundred and fifty dollars when you get back. When you talking about opening up, anyway?"

"Today's Tuesday, so by Friday. Why?"

"Just wanted to know when I can expect the rest of my money, that's all."

"You'll get it Friday, alright. But I might need a key to your apartment."

"What you need a key to my apartment for?"

"In case you ain't here and I need to get in to get my shit."

"Oh don't worry, you gon' be able to get in, just make sure you got my money."

"Yeah alright, but anyway, I'm gon' get out of here 'cause I got some other shit to do."

"Ok," Sonya replied, and as soon as Spoon walked out, all she could think about was how she was going to get him back.

***

Standing in his living room, Moose could feel his anger rising as he looked around at the damage that had been done. His couches were turned over, pictures snatched from the walls, lamps broken, and they even broke his fish tank. Sloshing through water, he stepped over broken furniture as he made his way down the hallway towards the bedrooms. Peaking inside, it looked as if a tornado had been through there. That's when he saw the bag at the foot of the bed. Rushing over to it, he pulled it open and saw his scale and cooking utensils still inside. Dropping the bag, he turned and sprinted across the hall to his bedroom and while navigating his way through everything that was thrown about, he made his way to the closet. Looking inside, he knew they'd gotten the dope. Then remembering Ms. Marshall saying that she saw one of the two boys carrying a bag when they left, he rushed back outside.

"Ms. Marshall," he said while walking to the gate.

"Yes, young man," she replied.

"Those two men you saw, how old would you say they were?"

"Oh about eighteen or nineteen, if I had to guess."

"Do you recall ever seeing them before?"

"Well you know with the park being right across the street, it could've been some of the neighborhood kids."

"Yeah, that's what I thought, too." Moose replied.

"Did they take anything important?" Ms. Marshall asked.

"Oh yeah," he thought to himself, *"But what I'm gon' give 'em when I catch 'em ain't gon' be nothing nice, I can promise you that."*

CHAPTER 7

Arriving back home from their dinner engagement, Wesley and Carla boarded the elevator and pressed the button for the top floor. As soon as the doors closed, he pushed her up against the wall, reached under her skirt, and began pulling her panties to the side.

"Wesley, what are you doing?" Carla squealed while grabbing his hand.

"I'm showing you how to live a little," he replied.

"Here in the elevator? What if someone sees us?"

"There's no one here but us."

"Well why can't we wait till we get upstairs?"

"You said you were willing to try new things, right?"

"Yes, but in the elevator?"

"Yes, in the elevator," he answered while reaching out to stop the elevator in-between floors.

"Wesley, you can't—"

"I can't what?" He said looking directly at her.

"What if someone wants to get on the elevator?"

"They can wait, now are you willing to try new things with me or not?"

"Yes, but..."

"But what, Carla?"

"Yes, Wesley, I just want to make you happy."

"Then relax and let me show you what you've been missing."

Reaching up, he began unbuttoning her blouse as she leaned back and closed her eyes. After unsnapping her bra to reveal her perky breast, he bent down to take one of her nipples in his mouth. Carla sighed as he nibbled one then the other while reaching his hand under her skirt. Pulling her panties to the side, he began gently rubbing his hand back and forth across her neatly trimmed pussy. Carla felt herself becoming wetter as Wesley suddenly slid his finger inside of her, and as he began fingering her, he continued nibbling on her breast.

"Oh God! What am I doing?" She thought to herself as Wesley kissed her passionately while pulling her skirt up over her hips and suddenly feeling exposed, she kissed him back hungrily.

Kneeling down in front of her, he caught her totally off guard and before she could utter a word, he buried his face between her legs. Spreading her legs further, he flicked his tongue back and forth across her clitoris and unable to believe that she was getting her pussy eaten in an elevator, she looked down at him to make sure she wasn't dreaming. Closing her eyes, she threw her head back as Wesley continued to lick and suck her pussy with abandon.

It amazed Wesley that all it took was for him to put his foot down to get her to open up and although he loved her deeply, he planned to take full advantage of it. Continuing to lick and suck, Wesley reached up to caress her ass while pulling her to him. Then, while gently nibbling on her clitoris, she came.

"Oh, God! Wesley, I'm coming," she said, stifling her screams as he continued eating her hungrily.

He stood and kissed her passionately, and tasting herself on his lips, she became more aroused. Breaking their embrace, he smiled, "Now was that so bad?"

"No, but I can't believe you got me doing this in an elevator," she replied while fixing her clothes.

"Oh, that's only the beginning," he said before pushing the button to release the elevator. "Wait till I get you in the apartment."

"But…"

"Shh!" Wesley said cutting her off and as the elevator doors opened, they stepped off into the apartment. Suddenly turning to face her, he began removing her clothes.

"What are you doing?"

"I'm taking your clothes off."

"I know that, but why? You know one is good enough for me."

"Yeah, but it's all about trying new things, right?"

"Yeah, but wasn't the elevator thing enough?"

"No. Now relax. I'm sure you won't be disappointed."

Having removed all of her clothes, Wesley then stepped back and began undressing and assuming a round of sex was coming, Carla laid back on the couch, spread her legs, and waited.

"Not like that," Wesley said while looking down at her.

Carla started to protest, but suddenly remembering what she'd said about trying new things, she thought better of it. "Ok, what do you want me to do?"

"Get on all fours with your ass facing me," he replied, and as she complied, he positioned himself behind her, grabbed her hips, and rubbed his dick back and forth across her moist pussy.

Still sensitive from her first orgasm, Carla buried her face in the pillow. Then without warning, Wesley positioned himself at her opening before burying himself deep inside of her. Up until tonight, the only position they'd tried was missionary and while it was fulfilling, for some reason this position made him seem bigger and longer. Gently massaging her ass, Wesley continued sliding his dick in and out of her warm, wet pussy while gradually increasing his pace.

Carla couldn't believe the feeling he was giving her as he slid in and out repeatedly. But after tonight, they would be using this position regularly. Continuing to fuck her with long, deep strokes, Wesley suddenly switched gears as he grabbed her waist, pulling her into him. Then while gripping her ass, he began pounding his dick in and out of her over and over again. Carla came again as he continuously pounded hard and fast and just when she thought it could get no better, she came again. Suddenly pulling out of her, he looked at her lustfully.

"What's wrong?" she asked looking back at him.

"Nothing, lay on your back," he replied and as Carla rolled onto her back and spread her legs, Wesley positioned himself between them and getting up on his toes, he braced himself and began sliding his dick in and out of her.

Carla watched as his dick disappeared inside of her and wondered how something could feel so good. Then reaching up to caress his face, she couldn't wait to find out what he would do next when suddenly without warning, she came again as he submerged himself deep inside of her and grabbing him tight, she threw her head back and moaned with pleasure.

"Three times in one night," Wesley thought to himself as he continued pounding his dick in and out of her. That was a record for them and he was far from being through.

While enjoying the pleasure he gave, Carla thought about the countless times she'd told him, "Not like that Wesley," or "Not right here," and realized that she'd been depriving herself. Well not anymore, because if he was going to make her feel how she was feeling now, he could get it any way he wanted to. Suddenly, she felt his body stiffen and with one last thrust, he came. Finally slipping out of her, Wesley took a seat next to her.

"I don't hear you complaining now," he said with a smile.

"Ain't nothing to complain about," she replied while punching him playfully.

"Oh, really! Well let's see, you got your pussy sucked in an elevator, you've managed to come three times tonight already, and..."

"Ok," she said cutting him off. "And it definitely wasn't how I thought it was gon' be."

"What did you expect?"

"I don't know, but you know I always thought only women who were whores did stuff like that."

"Now why would you think that?" Wesley asked smiling.

"It's just how I was raised, that's all. I mean, when someone tells you that only whores do this and that, after a while, you start believing it."

"Do you still feel like that?"

"Well no, but I'll admit it's a lot different than what I'm used to."

"How so?"

"It felt good, for one," she replied smiling.

"Oh it did, huh?"

"Yeah, but what about you?"

"What do you mean?"

"Was it good for you? I mean, me loosening up and all."

"Hell yeah, but I want you to understand something. When a man loves a woman, there's nothing he won't do for her, and vice versa."

"I'm not sharing you, Wesley."

"No not anything like that, 'cause I damn sure ain't sharing you. But I mean like, together you and me, for instance, I sucked your pussy because you're my woman and I love you. Oh, and you taste good, too."

"I love you, too," she replied smiling. "But I don't know how to do all those things."

"What things are you talking about?"

"You know, like sucking on you and the things you like."

"That's ok."

"But I want to make you happy."

"I am happy Carla, and as far as those other things, you can learn if you're willing."

"Haven't I proven that I am?"

"Yeah, well get ready for your next lesson."

***

"Alright y'all listen up," Spoon said after walking in the house to see Germ and Clarence talking to a man he didn't know.

"Hey, this my cousin who I was telling you about," Clarence replied. "You know, about cooking the work."

"Oh yeah, what's up?"

"He say he can do it for a grand."

"The whole quarter key?"

"Yeah and I'll get you ten ounces instead of nine," Clarence's cousin suddenly said.

"Shit, when can you start?"

"Right now, if you want me to. Just have my money when I'm done."

"That ain't no problem, but I want to see the first two ounces. If they straight, we'll pay you to cook all the work we get."

"Alright, but trust me, all your shit gon' be straight."

"Hey Germ, you got the shit you were supposed to get?"

"Yeah man, I got it."

"Alright then, let's see it."

Pulling out a bag, Germ opened it and began removing a scale and bags of various sizes.

"Hey, what's your cousin's name?"

"We call him Shorty Fats."

"Yeah, what's up?" Shorty Fats asked.

"What you need to get started?"

"Oh, I got all my shit already, I'm just waiting for y'all to give me what y'all want cooked."

"Alright, just give me a minute," Spoon replied as he along with Clarence and Germ went inside of Clarence's room and locked the door.

"Germ, get the half a key out the bag so we can weigh this shit out," Spoon said and as Germ went to get the dope, they all waited anxiously.

"You know how much a quarter's supposed to weigh?" Clarence asked.

"Yeah, don't you?"

"Nah, that's why I'm asking you."

"Well it's supposed to be two hundred and fifty two grams, but most people weigh it out at two fifty."

As Germ brought the half a key over, Spoon pulled out the scale. After grabbing one of the plastic bags, he proceeded to weigh out two hundred and fifty grams of coke. Tying the bag closed, he weighed out the other quarter and it too weighed two hundred and fifty.

"Alright, check it," Spoon said. "We need to find somewhere safe to stash these four keys, 'cause we can't afford to have Clarence's ole woman find 'em. I'm gon' give Shorty Fats this shit so he can start cooking and we can keep the other quarter here till we need it. Oh yeah, and the broad I told y'all about in the apartments, she wit' it but it's gon' cost us five hundred dollars a month to stash our shit there. I gave her two fifty today and told her she'd get the rest on Friday when we open up shop, so y'all owe me eighty dollars apiece, plus three hundred dollars for Clarence's cousin."

"Damn man, a nigga ain't gon' have shit left," Germ complained.

"What the fuck you crying for?" Spoon replied, "After you give me the three hundred dollars, you'll still have at least five hundred dollars and you ain't had that this morning. Besides, you gotta spend money to make money."

"Here's mine," Clarence said while handing Spoon his share. "'Cause I know we gon' get it back plus some."

After receiving Germ's share of the money, Spoon went out and handed the work to Shorty Fats who immediately got to work. As he was setting up, he eyed the bag carefully. "This the whole bag?"

"Yeah, why, what's up?" Spoon replied.

"Oh, I just wanted to know 'cause depending on how good the coke is, all of 'em should come back twenty seven point five grams."

"Shit, that'll be straight," Spoon said and as Shorty Fats got to work, he and the others sat wondering about all the money they were going to make.

CHAPTER 8

"Like that?" Carla asked while kneeling between Wesley's legs.

"Yeah, that's good, just keep licking it like you would some ice cream then put it in your mouth."

"I can't fit all this in my mouth."

"That's alright, just put a little bit of it in until you get used to it, but make sure you don't scrape it with your teeth 'cause that shit hurts."

"Ok," she said as she began licking up and down the sides of his dick. Then forming an circle with her mouth, she took him in. Concentrating on licking and sucking the head, she gauged his reaction and hearing him moan, she began taking more of him in her mouth. Although it was her first time, she liked the feeling of his dick rubbing back and forth across the roof of her mouth and wanting so much to please him, she lowered her head until she felt him in the back of her throat. Suddenly gagging, she came up for air.

"I can't do it."

"Yes you can," he replied trying to soothe her. "Remember how you sucked on my finger?"

"Yeah, but that was your finger, this is bigger," she said while massaging him up and down.

"I know, but you do it the same way."

"I'm trying."

"Listen, I know it's your first time so I don't expect you to be perfect."

"But I want to do it like you like it, I just don't know how."

"You'll learn, you just have to be patient and you have to practice."

"Alright," Carla replied. "But I want to learn to do it better than anybody has ever done it to you."

"Then do it like you did my finger, but this time just concentrate on the head."

"Alright," she said as she took him back in her mouth. Wesley leaned back on the couch and watched as Carla licked, teased and sucked his dick and as soon as he closed his eyes, he heard the phone ring.

"Damn!" he thought to himself as he looked down at Carla who was still at work. With the phone still ringing, he couldn't concentrate, so he leaned forward.

"Wait a minute! That may be important," he said before answering it, and while listening to him speak she felt insecure. In her mind, if she was doing it the way she was supposed to, the last thing he'd have been worrying about was answering the phone.

"Hold up! Did you just say that somebody broke into your house?"

"Yeah, man."

"Somebody like who?"

"I don't know, but my neighbor says she saw two young cats in my yard so it's probably some teenagers from the neighborhood."

"Ok, but what about the shit I gave you?"

"Well, remember I told you I still had a half a key left form the other shit?"

"Yeah, I remember."

"Well when you left, I cooked up two of the keys, then I made the rounds dropping everything off. When I got back, my back door was kicked in and the shit's gone."

"You mean to tell me that some ma'fuckin' kids walking 'round with my shit?" Wesley screamed.

"So far, that's what it's looking like." Moose replied.

"How much of it did they get?"

"Four and a half keys."

"Fuck!" Wesley screamed, startling Carla while jumping to his feet. "I'm on my way," he said before slamming down the phone and storming off towards the room."

Carla had seen him upset before, *"but never like this,"* she thought while following him to the room.

"Baby, what's wrong?"

"I've got to go handle something," he replied while putting on his clothes.

"You want me to come with you?"

"No, just stay here and I'll be back."

"But Wesley, I…"

"Look," he said turning to face her, "I said I got something to go take care of and I want you to stay here till I get back, alright?"

Nodding her head, Carla stood frozen in place as Wesley finished getting dressed. Then after grabbing his keys off the dresser, he kissed her on the cheek and was out the door without another word. For several minutes, Carla sat trying to figure what had just happened. She'd seen him transform right before her eyes and it was like he'd become another person. Although he'd never given her reason to be afraid of him, it puzzled her because what could this Moose person have said to make him that upset? She'd have to ask him when he got home, but right now she needed to see her friend Sheila and maybe get a few tips on how to please her man.

Meanwhile, Wesley drove like a maniac on his way to Moose's house and the more he thought about somebody breaking into his friend's place and running off with his dope, the madder he got. Finally turning the corner, he drove down the street towards his friend's house while looking at the youngsters in the park. "One of you ma'fuckers got my shit," he said to himself. "But trust me, I'm gon' get it back in blood."

Coming to a stop in front of Moose's house, he parked, got out, and walked to the door and before he could knock, Moose was already opening the door.

"Damn!" he said as he stepped inside and looked around at all the damage. "Two kids did all this?"

"That's what my neighbor said she saw."

"Well, put the word out that I'll give ten grand to anybody who can tell us who did this."

"I already called around and told everybody to be on the lookout for anybody trying to get rid of it."

"Yeah, well maybe ten grand will make 'em move faster. What else did they take?"

"Nothing, just tore my shit up."

"Hey man, I know it's fucked up but all this shit can be replaced."

"Yeah, but what about the work?"

"Oh, don't worry 'bout it, I'll have six more for you by tomorrow. Regardless of that, we gon' find the ma'fuckers who broke into your shit. I don't give a fuck if they're old or young, they took something from me and I want it back. Nobody's ever taken anything from me and lived to talk about it.

"Look man, I'm sorry," Moose said, "If I hadn't left it here…"

"Man, hold up! What you sorry for? You didn't take the shit so you ain't got nothing to be sorry for."

"Yeah, but I mean—"

"Listen," Wesley said cutting him off, "we've been friends for, what, twenty five years now?"

"Yeah, 'bout that."

"We've made money together and lost it together but no matter what, we always came out on top. You know why?"

"'Cause you know I'll ride or die with you."

"That too," Wesley shot back, "but besides that, we're friends first. Everything else is secondary."

"Yeah man, but shit done changed. These young niggas nowadays ain't got no respect for nobody. They think they can just do what they want to do and consequences be damned."

"Yeah, I feel you," Wesley replied, "'Cause back in the days, a nigga never would've tried this shit."

"Yeah, 'cause his whole family would've been dead by now."

"Damn right, but you know what? Sometimes that's all a nigga respect."

"What you mean?" Moose asked.

"I mean when Hood was out there handling his business, niggas stayed in check, but he hasn't put in work in a minute."

"So what are you thinking?"

"Put it like this, life is full of examples and sometimes you gotta make one or become one. I think it's time we make one."

"Do you really want to do that and jeopardize what you've worked so hard to build?"

"Moose, listen to me. I was Hood when you met me and regardless of what happened inbetween then and now, I'm still Hood. I didn't get to where I am by rolling over and being a bitch for nobody and I ain't about to start now. Somebody came in here and took my shit and if they don't give a fuck, I don't give a fuck either. When people see me now, they see Mr. Wesley, but I think it's time for them to see that the Hood still ain't nothing nice. Now here's what we're gonna do."

***

Pulling up to her friend's apartment building on 136th street and N.E. 6th Avenue, Carla sat in her car contemplating whether to go through with her plan or not. Her friend Sheila had men eating out of the palm of her hand and when Carla asked what her secret was, she replied, "To keep a man, you have to be a lady in the streets and a freak in the sheets." At the time Carla didn't give it much thought, but now that she was willing to explore new things, who better to ask?

After finally making up her mind, she got out the car and climbed the flight of stairs leading to her friend's apartment. Once she was at the top, she slowly made her way down the hall until she reached Sheila's door. Nervously, she knocked and seconds later, her friend answered. "Girl, what you doing over here?"

"I came to ask a favor," Carla replied.

"Girl, come on in and tell me what's on your mind," her friend said and as Carla stepped through the door, Sheila closed and locked it. "You're a long way from home, ain't you?"

"Look, I admit that I tended to look at things differently than most people, but I had a revelation recently and it sort of got me looking at things from a new perspective."

"Oh, really now?" Sheila said with a smirk. "Well, tell me about the revelation that got you looking at things from, as you say, a new perspective."

"You're not gonna make this easy, are you?"

"No, because I want to know what got Ms. Goody Two Shoes over here to ask me for a favor."

"Ok, remember the time I asked you how it is that you got all these guys wrapped around your finger?"

"Yeah, and do you remember what I told you?"

"Yeah, and I got the lady part down. I need you to teach me how to be a freak in the sheets."

"Wait a minute!" Sheila said. "Did you just say you want me to teach you how to be a freak?"

"Yeah I, uh, remember how you use to tell me about all the things you used to do to make a man unable to resist you and I thought…"

"Thought what?" 'Cause I just don't see somebody as uptight as you doing those things."

"Well for starters, I got my pussy eaten for the first time in an elevator and I kind of liked it."

"What!" Sheila screamed. "When? By who?"

"By Wesley, tonight after we came back from dinner."

"And just how did he get you to try that?"

"He told me how he wanted to try new things with me and I agreed, so we did it in the elevator."

"Damn girl, I ain't never had my pussy eaten in an elevator. Is that all he did?"

"No, I let him fuck me in different positions and believe me, it felt so good. That's why I decided to ask you to teach me a few things so I can rock his world."

"Oh trust me Carla, you'll do more than rock his world. After I'm through with you, you'll literally blow his mind."

CHAPTER 9

"Ms. Conyers."

"Yes, Ms. Summer?"

"Could you get me the number for Commissioner Mitchell, please?"

"No problem, it'll take just a minute."

As she sat at her desk waiting for her secretary to get the number, Assistant State Attorney Eyvette Summers thought about Brad Wesley. Ever since seeing him at the dinner, images of his handsome face and chocolate skin flashed through her mind. There was just something about the way he carried himself that piqued her interest, and waking up after dreaming about him didn't make it any easier. Being an Assistant State Attorney in Miami Dade County for the past ten years, she'd prosecuted her share of cases, but with the rise in juvenile offenders being prosecuted in adult courts, she began to question her choice of career. With a teenage son of her own, she realized that most of them were just kids making stupid mistakes and while there were a few genuinely bad ones, she reasoned that with a little guidance most of them could be saved. Attending the dinner, she'd listened as Brad Wesley talked about not giving up on them and to do so would mean that the older generation had failed and she was quite impressed. It also didn't hurt that he was good looking and had money. Staring at him from across the room, he had an aura about himself that commanded attention and as she sat behind her desk, she smiled to herself and thought, *"Well Mr. Wesley, you definitely have mine."*

Suddenly brought back to the present as her secretary entered her office, Eyvette looked up at her.

"Here's the number you asked for."

"Oh, thank you Rachel and please close the door on your way out," she replied and while waiting for her secretary to leave, she stared at the number.

Her and Bob Mitchell had worked together after a surge of shootings gripped the Liberty City Area and although they weren't considered friends, it wouldn't seem out of the ordinary for her to call him inquiring about Wesley, considering his contributions towards ending youth violence. Picking up the phone, she dialed the number and waited, and seconds later a voice on the other end answered, "County Commissioners office, how may I help you?"

"Yes, this is Eyvette Summers from the State Attorney's office. May I please speak with Commissioner Mitchell?"

"One moment please," the voice replied before putting her on hold.

Seconds later, the Commissioner came on the line, "Ms. Summers, what can I do for you?"

"Hi Bob, I don't mean to disturb you but I was wondering if you could help me in contacting the guest speaker you had at the fundraiser last night?"

"Oh, you're talking about Brad Wesley?"

"Yeah that's his name, I want to ask him if he'd mind speaking at our next youth conference. I was so moved by his speech last night and thought it would be a good idea if he could."

"Mr. Wesley is a fine gentleman," the Commissioner replied. "And he's passionate about saving our young generation with the sponsoring of youth centers and programs. I'm sure he'd be happy to speak to the kids, so please hold while I get the number."

While on hold, Eyvette thought about what she was going to say to Wesley. There really wasn't a youth conference, but she couldn't tell the Commissioner, "Hey I might want to fuck him."

"Ah, Ms. Summers!" The Commissioner said, coming back on the line.

"Yes Commissioner, I'm here."

"Ok, the number is three two five, four seven zero eight, you got that?"

"Yes, I got it and thank you, Mr. Mitchell."

"No problem Ms. Summers, anytime I can help, feel free to call me."

"Alright Mr. Mitchell, and thanks again, you have a nice day."

"You too, Ms. Summers."

"Ok, bye!" she said before hanging up. *"Now what do I say? Oh come on Eyvette, stop acting like some scared little school girl."* She thought to herself. Then quickly calming her nerves, she picked up the phone and dialed Wesley's number. Almost immediately, she heard the deep voice come on the line.

"Brokerage firm of Cohen and Williams, Brad Wesley speaking."

"Yes," she replied nervously. "This is Eyvette Summers from the State Attorney's office."

"How may I help you, Ms. Summers?"

"Damn, why does he have to sound so sexy?" she thought to herself. "Well, I got your number from Bob Mitchell and I was wondering if you and I could arrange a meeting to discuss your thoughts on possible diversion programs for youthful offenders?"

"Ms. Summers, while I support helping our youth, I'm no expert."

"I know, but I attended the dinner and heard what you said about not giving up on the younger generation. Me being a single mom of an eighteen year old son, I thought maybe we could sit down together and I could hear your thoughts on what can be done to curb youth violence..."

"Didn't you say that you're calling from the State Attorney's office?"

"Yes I am, and I see so many young black kids come in the courtroom and get caught up in the system. That's why, after hearing you speak at the dinner, I thought maybe we could sit down and discuss other alternatives than just locking them up."

"In that case, Ms. Summers, I'd love to sit down with you and discuss possibilities," Wesley replied.

"Good, and when would it be convenient for you?"

"Well, I'm always free in the evenings. So any time after six would be fine."

"Ok, let's say this Friday at around seven?"

"That's fine," Wesley replied. "Just tell me where to meet you."

"How about you pick the location."

"Ok, how does the Olive Garden on one sixty third street and northeast second avenue sound?"

"Sounds wonderful," Eyvette replied. "So I guess I'll see you on Friday at seven."

"Yes, and I look forward to meeting you there."

"Likewise, Mr. Wesley."

Hanging up the phone, Eyvette smiled from ear to ear while going over the conversation in her head. His voice alone aroused her and she became moist as she anticipated seeing him. The hard part was over, she thought. She'd gotten him to meet with her, now all she had to do was figure out what to wear.

***

Meanwhile, back at Clarence's house, all the dope was cooked and bagged and they stood in Clarence's kitchen contemplating their next move.

"Alright listen," Spoon suddenly said. "Once we get rid of this, we'd have made nine thousand dollars. I'm gon' give each of ya'll two thousand dollars apiece."

"Man, hold up!" Germ screamed, "I thought we're supposed to split everything three ways."

"Well there's been a change of plans," Spoon replied.

"First of all, it was my idea and if it wasn't for me, both of y'all niggas would still be broke."

"Yeah, but I went in the house with you," Germ said. "So by right, half of that shit is mine."

"Nigga, you ain't getting half of shit," Spoon shot back menacingly. "You didn't even want to go in the ma'fucka, talking 'bout what that nigga Hood gon' do to us. Now if you don't want the two grand, let me know now and I'll find somebody else."

"Damn man, you ain't gotta act like that. I mean, I'm good, I just thought…"

"Well stop thinking 'cause I'm running this shit," Spoon replied. "Besides, y'all getting the two grand for just being down with a nigga."

"Well I ain't complaining 'bout the money," Clarence said. "I'm just glad I'm down with y'all. At least now a nigga will have some money in his pockets."

"Look, y'all ain't got nothing to worry 'bout. I'm tryin' to get this shit jumpin' so all us can eat, you feel me?"

"Hell yeah, but when we supposed to open up shop?" Germ asked.

"Well I told Sonya Friday, but since we got all the shit ready, I'm thinkin' 'bout opening up tomorrow."

"Shit, why not? I mean, what else we got to do?"

"Honestly, nothing," Spoon replied. "So here's what we'll do. I'll serve the work while Germ collects the money."

"What about me?" Clarence asked.

"You keep the gun and you gon' deal with any problems we might have. Think you can handle that?"

"Hell yeah, and a nigga better not come round here with the bullshit or I'll make an example out of his ass."

"Alright then, so it's set, y'all just be ready to put in work tomorrow. In the meantime, Clarence, make sure you stash that work good 'cause we don't need your old woman finding that."

"Shit, I'll be in trouble for real," Clarence screamed. "But don't worry, I got that. I'll put it somewhere safe where we won't have to worry 'bout nobody taking it from us."

"Yeah, and we'll meet you over here in the morning," Spoon replied.

"Alright, that'll work, you just bring that heat, nigga."

"Oh, I got that," Spoon said before heading for the door and after walking out, he closed the door behind him.

CHAPTER 10

Carla was up bright and early. Wesley had already left for work and the apartment was quiet. The night before, he'd returned home and didn't say a word about where he'd been or why and she didn't ask. Instead, he took a shower, climbed into bed and slept, leaving her wondering. As she lay there staring at the ceiling, images of him and another woman flashed through her mind and she thought about what her friend had told her. *"If your man can't get it at home, he'll find it in the streets."* Climbing out of bed, she put on a robe and headed to the kitchen where she'd left the items her friend had given her. Reaching under the sink, she removed a bag, turned, and walked into the living room. In the bag was a porno tape compliments of her friend Sheila, who told her to watch it and then emulate what she saw. Also in the bag was an eight and a half-inch dildo, and while it did look a bit intimidating, it wasn't like her to just suck anyone's dick, so it offered her the practice she needed.

After removing the tape, she walked over and popped it in the player before pressing play. Then taking a seat on the couch, she watched as the images filled the screen. It showed a man and a woman in the shower with the man standing and the woman on her knees in front of him. She was amazed to see the woman taking him in and out of her mouth with such ease and knew that the only way she'd be able to do that same thing to Wesley was if she practiced. Removing the dildo from the bag, she sat staring at it for several minutes and figuring Wesley was about that size, she knew that if she learned to swallow the whole dildo, then doing it to Wesley would be a breeze. Looking back at the TV screen, she listened to the sounds the man made as the woman took him in and out of her mouth, and with one last thought she slid the dildo between her lips. For the next hour and a half, she licked and sucked on the dildo just as she'd seen the woman on the screen do, and although she couldn't take it all the way in, she was pleased with her progress. Grabbing the remote, she rewound the tape to the beginning, then placing the dildo upright on the glass table she got down on her knees in front of it, and with one last look at the screen, she took it to the back in her throat.

***

Moose spent the first part of the day getting his house in order, and by the time twelve o'clock rolled around he was only half finished. Taking a break, he sat down and began to think about his conversation with Wesley. It's been a while since Hood ran the streets, but now because of the recent break in, he was about to do just that. He thought about the last time they'd gone to war. Some Italians had come to Miami with the purpose of taking over, but what they didn't expect was that when dealing with the Hood, anything could happen. When diplomacy didn't work, Hood declared war, and although they'd lost some good men and Hood had gotten shot, when the dust settled he was the last man standing.

Running them out of town was the easy part, but then the feds came and Hood had to go underground. He enrolled in school, got a degree, and now he works for a prestigious brokerage firm, all the while hiding in plain sight. Moose liked to be able to come and go as he pleased without having to look over his shoulder, and now that the feds were off their trail, he was able to enjoy the simple pleasures life had to offer. With this new situation, he knew that was all about to change because he had a strange feeling that things were about to get heated. With no word yet on who broke into his house, all they could do was wait patiently for whoever it was to make a mistake. There was no way anyone could sit on that amount of dope because the allure of money was just too strong, especially in times like this. Wesley would be by tonight with more and he had to get ready. After standing, he got back to cleaning the house.

***

Back in the conference room of Cohen and Williams, Wesley sat discussing proposals with a representative of the Dana Corporation.

"Mr. Wesley, we are willing to offer your company fifty million dollars as a down payment on the one sixty fifth street mall and another fifty million when the renovations are complete."

"Mr. Cox, while that is a substantial amount of money, I'm not inclined to accept your offer at this time."

"And why is that, may I ask?"

"Well, reports from the Federal Reserve show weaker than expected sales and flagging consumer confidence, overshadowing an upbeat view of the economy. This week's consumer report was a shock for traders about exactly how uncomfortable consumers still are with their finances and the state of the economy. One of the biggest worries for people in the job market and with unemployment still rising is that it's hard to expect progress. Now, I could agree to your proposal and be done with it, but not only am I here to make money, I'm here to make sure my clients make money. Just for argument's sake, say I accepted your proposal, then unemployment continues to rise and consumer confidence stays low. Do you think people will be rushing to spend their hard earned money in the mall?"

"Well, no…" Mr. Cox replied.

"My point exactly, and while we would have made a substantial profit, you, or should I say the Dana Corporation, will lose money in the long run."

"Well, I'm sure that the people I represent will be glad to know that you have their best interest in mind."

"Mr. Cox," Wesley said while leaning forward. "This company has been in business for over fifty years and you know why? Because we're in business to help our clients make money and when they do, it ensures future business. Now, in six months, as consumer confidence builds and the job market shows improvement, I'm certain that we can get this deal done. If you insist on doing it now after hearing the facts, at least you know what to expect."

"I, ah, think I'll wait and talk to my colleagues before I sign off on the deal. But I want to thank you for being up front and I look forward to doing business with you in the future."

"And so do I," Wesley replied. "Now if you excuse me, I have a very important call to make. My secretary will see you out."

"Ok, and again, thank you," Mr. Cox replied before walking out, and while watching him go, Wesley thought about Ms. Summers and decided to give Moose a call to find out if he'd heard anything. He also had to stop by Moose's house later to drop off some more work, but right now he had to inform his boss of the development of the meeting.

Walking down the hall to his boss's office, Wesley entered to find him on the phone and after taking a seat, he waited. Seconds later, his boss hung up and looked across the desk at him.

"So, how did it go?"

"I turned down the deal," Wesley replied.

"You did what?!"

"Now calm down before—"

"No you listen to me Wesley, that was a hundred million dollar deal, and you turned it down! What were you thinking?"

"Well, I told you my intention was to make 'em sweat."

"Make them sweat! Shit, you're gonna give me a fucking heart attack."

"Alright, but just listen. In six months, we'll come back to the table and the deal will be worth more."

"How so?"

"Consumer spending will be up and the unemployment rate will have leveled off, meaning more businesses will begin hiring again so the deal will be worth more. I was thinking that maybe I can offer a counterclaim of, say, one hundred and twenty million, twenty million dollars more than what they're offering now."

"And that's because consumers will have gone back to spending rather than sitting on their money?"

"Exactly," Wesley replied with a smile.

"What's to say that they won't change their mind?"

"Because, as I explained to Mr. Cox, we could've signed off on the deal, got our money, and called it a day. At the same time, they'd be losing money."

"Because of the economy."

"Right, but this way we both gain, we come away with an extra twenty million dollars, and they reap the benefits of people filing up their mall and spending their hard earned money."

"It's a risky move, but I like it," his boss replied.

"Have I ever let you down?"

"No, but you scare the hell out of me sometimes."

"Boss," Wesley said with a smile, "sometimes I scare myself."

CHAPTER 11

Sonya sat in the tub after taking her daughter to daycare. Ever since Spoon had come around, talking about his own spot in the apartment, thoughts of him stayed in her mind. She'd met him her ninth grade year in high school and back then, he seemed so cute. Although he didn't have much at the time, he paid attention to her. After graduation, she'd moved out of her mom's house and reality quickly set in. She had bills to pay and with Spoon having no job or money, they argued constantly before they eventually drifted apart. Now years later, he was back with a pocket full of money and talking about opening his own spot. Yeah, things definitely had changed since the last time she'd seen him.

At the age of twenty one, Sonya still looked good despite having a three year old daughter. At five feet and two inches tall and weighing 135 pounds, she was always the center of attention and not only because of her dark complexion and fat ass. With her shoulder length hair and model features, she was considered beautiful by any standard. But what made her stand out was her no-nonsense attitude. She could get along with anyone, male or female, but if you crossed her you'd have hell on your hands 'cause she'd get down with the best of them. When she first moved into her apartment, all eyes were on her which made some of the females jealous, but when one of them got the nerve to step up to her and ended up needing a hundred and fifty stitches, everyone steered clear of the crazy bitch in apartment 222.

Stepping out of the tub, she began drying off when she heard somebody knocking on her door. Wrapping herself in a towel, she went to see who it was and looking through the peep hole, she saw that it was Spoon. Opening the door, she saw him standing there in a pair of Timberlands and an all-white t-shirt. *"Damn, he looks good"* she thought to herself, then suddenly looking directly at him she spoke, "Today's Thursday, Spoon, you said you'd be back Friday. So what you want?"

"Damn! Why you always got to be trippin' when a nigga come by here?" Spoon replied.

"'Cause I know you be with the bullshit."

"Look, I know I told you Friday, but I decided to open up shop a day early."

"So you brought my money?"

"Yeah, I brought your damn money, now you gon' let me in or what?"

"I ain't playing Spoon, I want my money," she replied while stepping aside to let him in and after closing the door behind him, she turned to face him. "I'm waitin'."

"Damn! Give me a minute, I told you I got it." Spoon replied as she stood with her hand on her hip, and reaching into his pocket he pulled out a wad of cash.

After quickly counting out her money, he handed it to her before putting the rest of the money back in his pocket.

"You satisfied now?" He asked while eyeing the towel she had wrapped around her.

"Yeah, I'm satisfied."

"Alright, where can I stash this shit?"

"Stash what?"

"What we talked about the other day."

"How much shit you got?"

"What difference does it make?"

"'Cause I need to know what's in my shit."

"Well it ain't nothing but nine ounces."

"Boy, you walking 'round with all that dope? You got to be crazy."

"Why you think I'm paying you?" Spoon replied. "So I won't have to be walking round with it. Now you gon' tell me where I can put it or what?"

"Yeah, boy come on, you can put it in my room." Sonya said before walking off and smiling to herself. Spoon followed.

"You can put it in the closet, I'll just keep my daughter out of here."

"Alright," Spoon replied and as he brushed past her, she could smell his cologne.

Unzipping the bag, he removed two ounces before closing it and placing the bag in the back of the closet.

Closing the door, he turned suddenly and caught her staring at him. "What?"

"I ain't said nothing."

"Well, why you looking at me like that?"

"Like what?"

"I don't know, like you got something on your mind."

"Nah I'm good, just checking out how much you done changed since the last time I saw you."

"Shit! You the one done changed," he replied while stepping closer to her. "You grown now, got a baby and all."

"Yeah, well it was supposed to be yours if you would've acted right."

"You know what, I ain't even gon' go there with you."

"Why, 'cause you know I'm right, don't you?"

"Sonya, we were young and I just wasn't ready for those type of responsibilities."

"Nah, you just wanted to run the streets with your homeboys instead of handling your business at home."

"Ok, but what does that have to do with right now?" he asked with his face just inches from hers.

"Nothin', I'm just saying."

"Well, right now I'm trying to get some money, I ain't got all day to stand around arguing with you about something that happened three years ago."

"You're right and I apologize." She replied.

"It's cool but remember this, you can't never move forward if you're always looking back, you feel me?"

Sonya nodded her head in understanding as Spoon eyed her closely. Then catching her off guard, he kissed her. Surprised by this, Sonya reached out to grab him to keep herself from falling as he pulled her into him. Unable to resist, she kissed him back while he massaged her ass gently. Pushing her back onto the bed, Spoon removed her towel and gazed down at her before leaning down to take one of her nipples in his mouth. Offering no resistance, Sonya loved the way he took control and let him have his way. Reaching up between her legs, he gently rubbed her pussy as she spread her legs wider. Then after kissing a trail down her stomach, he parted her pussy lips with his thumbs and buried his tongue inside of her pink flesh.

Sonya squirmed and whimpered as he licked and sucked her pussy and while enjoying his oral pleasure, she couldn't believe how turned on she'd become.

Spoon was determined to show her just how much he'd changed over the years. He wasn't the little boy she remembered from school. Instead, he was a grown man doing grown man things and from this day on, she'd know that he was running shit. Pushing her legs farther back, he continued to slide his tongue in and out of her while reaching up to pinch her hard nipples. Flicking his tongue back and forth across her clitoris, Spoon listened as she moaned with pleasure, then arching her back, she came. As Spoon swallowed her juices, Sonya couldn't believe that this was the same person who used to cringe when she asked for a kiss, yet here he was with his face buried between her legs.

Suddenly sitting up, she pushed him up and reached for his zipper and was puzzled when he grabbed her hand.

"What's wrong?" she asked while looking up at him.

"Nothing," he replied with a smile. "I just wanted to show you that I ain't the same little nigga from high school.

Now I gotta go get this paper, 'cause time is money, you feel me?"

"Mmm hmmm!" she said.

"Listen, as long as you stay straight with me, I'm gon' take care of you, alright?"

"Alright, but you ain't gotta worry about me, just watch out for these slimy ass hoes 'round here."

"Shit, if they know like I know, they'll stay the fuck from 'round me," he replied and without another word, he turned and walked out of the room.

Stunned, Sonya lay there thinking. *"Damn!"* as she heard the front door open and close. She couldn't believe how he'd taken control all of a sudden, but she liked it and it turned her on. Her pussy throbbed as she lay there thinking about Spoon and one thing she was certain of. Before the day was out, she'd show him that she wasn't that same little girl either.

CHAPTER 12

James and Rick were jack boys, plain and simple. It's what they did for a living and although they had yet to hit the big one, they did get lucky from time to time. Having just robbed two keys the night before in Broward County, all they were looking for was a quick come up, and getting rid of the two keys for $17,500 apiece was sure to do that. With keys going for $25,000, they had no idea the suspicion they brought on themselves. But pulling up into the parking lot of the McDonald's restaurant located on 183rd Street and 47th Avenue, they would soon find out.

Shortly after receiving the work from Wesley last night, Moose received a call informing him that someone was trying to sell two keys. After questioning the caller, he learned that the sellers were two young cats and they were getting rid of them for little to nothing. Moose informed the caller to set up a meeting and as he drove to the meeting place, his thoughts were on resolving this as quickly as possible. Pulling up in the McDonald's parking lot, Moose noticed the blue Grand Prix and knew that that was who he was here to meet. Two cars down, he noticed Wesley sitting in a Grey Nissan Maxima and was confident that things would go as planned. Parking his car, Moose got out and headed inside but not before looking back at the two occupants in the Grand Prix. Once inside, he walked to the counter, ordered his food, and waited.

"That's him." James said.

"How do you know?"

"Well, the ma'fucka we supposed to meet is supposed to be in a red truck, right?"

"Yeah, but that ma'fucka old, what he gon' do with two bricks?"

"I don't care," James replied. "All I know is his money spends like anybody else's. Alright look, I'm gon' go inside and check, you just sit tight till I get back, alright?"

"Yeah alright," Rick replied. "Just don't have a nigga sittin' out here all day."

As James got out and went inside, Rick sat nervously inside the car unaware that he was being watched. James, on the other hand, was now standing behind Moose in the line, shifting his weight nervously from one foot to the next.

Having seen him come in, Moose turned to look at him carefully before speaking. "Denise says you got something for sale."

"I might," James replied, momentarily caught off guard by his comment.

"Well, I'm going to have a seat and eat my breakfast, feel free to join me if you decide that you do."

Watching Moose walk off, James was now certain that he was right. Taking a seat next to the window, Moose could see the parking lot and what happened next.

Sitting nervously inside the car, Rick kept his eyes glued to the door of the restaurant and didn't notice Wesley easing up alongside his car until it was too late. When he did look up, Wesley was opening the back door and pointing a chrome behind his head.

"Make a sound and I'll blow your brains all over the windshield and keep your hands on the steering wheel," Wesley said while climbing inside and scared out of his mind, Rick did as he was told. Too scared to move, Rick looked at the old man in the rearview mirror and spoke nervously, "So you gon' tell me what you want?"

"Shut up, I ain't asked you to talk."

"Yeah, I know," but his words were cut short when he felt the barrel of the gun press up against the back of his head.

"I ain't gon' tell you again."

Inside, Moose smiled to himself as James came around the corner with his food before taking a seat at his table.

"So you got two keys you want to sell." Moose said matter-of-factly.

"How do I know you ain't the police?" James replied.

"'Cause the police wouldn't have a gun pointed at you under the table."

"Hey, what the fuck!"

"Shut up," Moose said cutting him off. "Now we're gonna get up and walk out that door."

"And if I don't?"

"I'll blow your ass away right here, it makes no difference to me."

"Well, I think you're bluffing," James said suddenly feeling brave, until he saw Moose's hand come from underneath the table pointing a gun inches from his face.

"Still think I'm bluffing?" Moose asked through gritted teeth.

"Nah, you made your point," James replied. "But my friend might get spooked if he sees a stranger coming towards the car."

"Oh don't worry 'bout him, I'm sure he'll be happy to see us, now get your ass up."

As James stood up and walked to the door, Moose followed close behind and as they both walked outside and approached the car, he saw his friend's face while noticing someone sitting in the back seat. They both walked around to the passenger side where Moose opened the door. "Get in," he said before watching James climb into the backseat and after getting in next to Rick, Moose pointed his gun at him.

"Drive," he said and as Rick drove out of the parking lot, all he could think of was, *"Damn! How did I get myself into this?"*

Moose ordered him to drive down 183rd Street and after approaching 37th Avenue they pulled into the parking lot of the Carol City Apartments and parked.

"We gon' get out and walk to the apartment, if anyone of y'all make a sound or try to run, you'll be dead before the police get here. Y'all understand?"

"Yeah," they both replied.

All four of them got out and headed towards the apartments. Once inside, they walked down the hallway before stopping in front of apartment 226 where Wesley knocked several times.

Immediately the door was opened and after being ordered inside, they were told to sit.

"Alright, where's the shit?" Wesley suddenly asked.

"You mean to tell me that y'all went through all this just to rob us?" James screamed.

"Ma'fucka, I asked you a question," Wesley said while pulling out his gun and pointing it at them.

"Hold up!" Rick screamed. "It's in the trunk."

"It better be," Wesley replied while handing Moose the keys and as soon as Moose walked out, Wesley turned back to face the two men. "Where did y'all get the dope?"

"What?!" Rick screamed puzzled by the question.

"Y'all trying to sell two keys, right?"

"Yeah."

"So where did y'all get 'em from?"

"Man, what's that got to do with anything?"

"Well for one, it'll determine whether y'all walk out of here alive."

"Damn man, y'all ain't got to kill us over no two keys."

"It ain't 'bout the dope, it's 'bout where y'all got it from."

"Man look," James said clearly shaken, "I don't know what's going on, but we ain't done nothing to you. Shit, we don't even know you."

Suddenly, Moose walked in and after locking the door behind him, he handed Wesley one of the packages. While inspecting it, Wesley immediately knew that it wasn't their missing dope.

"It ain't ours," he said looking at Moose.

"Alright, so now what?"

After thinking for a few minutes, he threw the keys to James and Rick. "Y'all can go, just find somewhere else to sell that shit."

"We can go?" James screamed. "Man, y'all done took us through all this shit and y'all ain't gon' even buy it?"

"Just get y'all's ass out of here before I change my mind," Wesley replied in frustration.

"Alright, but—"

"But nothing," Rick said cutting him off. Then grabbing his arm, he led James to the door, opened it, and stepped outside.

"Thought we got lucky there for a minute," Moose said, his voice full of disappointment.

"Yeah, I kind of thought so, too," Wesley replied. "But hey, it'll come, we just have to be patient."

"Come on, I got y'all," their friend Harry said as they all headed for the door and opening it Moose stepped out into the hall at the same moment Germ walked past.

"Oh shit!" Germ said to himself as he recognized Moose coming out of the apartment with two other men, *"What the fuck he doing 'round here?"* he thought. Did he know about them? He didn't know, but he wasn't taking no chances, so he went to go tell Spoon.

CHAPTER 13

The next day, Wesley sat behind his desk going over paperwork when he came across a few messages left by his secretary. One of them was from Ms. Summers who'd called to verify their meeting tomorrow night and looking at his watch, he wondered if she was still in. *"Only one way to find out,"* he figured as he picked up the phone and dialed her number. After several rings, someone answered, "State Attorney's Office. How may I help you?"

"Yes, is Ms. Summers in?

"May I ask who's calling?"

"This is Brad Wesley and I'm returning her call."

"Ok, one moment please."

While on hold, his thoughts drifted to Carla. It had been two days since he'd been intimate with her and he smiled as he thought about what he was going to do to her tonight.

Suddenly, Ms. Summers came on the line and brought him back to the present, "Mr. Wesley, how nice of you to call."

"Yes, I've been in meetings all day and I just received your message. Hope I'm not interrupting you."

"Oh no, I just managed to get a little free time myself, so it's alright. I called you earlier to make sure that our meeting was still on for tomorrow evening."

"Of course, nothing's changed. That's seven o'clock at the Olive Garden, right?"

"That's correct, and I look forward to our meeting. I just had a sixteen-year-old girl in my courtroom today for selling drugs at her high school, can you believe it?"

"Well, kids are growing up fast nowadays," Wesley replied.

"Yeah I know, but it has to be a way for us to convince them that what they do with their lives today affects what happens in their lives later on."

"Well I'm sure that if we put our heads together, we'll be able to come up with something."

"I sure hope so."

"Well I won't hold you up, like I said I'm just returning your phone call."

"Oh no problem Mr. Wesley, and again I look forward to meeting with you tomorrow night."

"Same here," Wesley replied, "and you have a nice day."

"You too, Mr. Wesley. Bye."

As he hung up, his mind drifted back to Carla and he decided to give her a call.

***

Back in the apartments, Germ rushed around the corner to where Spoon and Clarence sat talking on the stairs.

"Man, did y'all see that old ma'fucka?"

"Nigga, what the fuck you talkin' 'bout?" Spoon replied.

"Remember the old man whose house we broke into?"

"Yeah, what about him?"

"I just walked past him and two other old cats!"

"You just walked past him?" Spoon screamed. "Walked past him where?"

"Right around there." Germ replied while pointing in the direction he'd just come from.

"Did he see you?"

"Hell yeah, you think I'd be acting like this if he didn't?"

"Do you think he knew who you was?"

"He didn't act like it. I mean, he didn't say nothing, just kept talking to the two niggas who was with him."

"Damn! Why you think he 'round here?"

"Man, I don't know, you want me to go ask him?"

"Alright nigga, you ain't got to be getting all smart and shit. I'm just tryin' to figure out what he's doing round here."

"Man, fuck him," Clarence said while pulling the gun from his waist. "I'll murk his ass if he comes round here with the bullshit."

"Man, hold up! We ain't got but one gun and it's three of them."

"I told you that nigga Hood had all kinds of ma'fuckas working for him," Clarence said. "Them niggas had Carol City on lock for years."

"Well that was then, this is now," Spoon replied. "And ain't nobody gon' stop us from getting money. Do you remember what apartment they came out of?"

"Two twenty six I think, why?"

"Damn, that's four doors down from Sonya."

"You think she knows them?" Clarence asked.

"I don't know, but I'll ask. Alright listen, Germ I want you to go by the house and get the other guns."

"Why, what's up?"

"Nothing really, but until we figure out what's going on, we at least should be on point."

"Ok, I'm feelin' that," Germ replied. "But what y'all gon' do till I get back?"

"We gon' chill at Sonya's apartment. Besides, I'm almost out of work, so I need to re-up anyway."

"Alright, I'll holla at y'all in a few."

As Germ walked off, Spoon and Clarence walked to Sonya's apartment for more work and to wait till he got back.

***

Carla sat on the couch smiling to herself. After two days of practicing, she was now able to swallow the whole dildo without gagging and she couldn't wait to surprise Wesley with her new skill. As she thought about what his reaction would be, she heard the phone ring and rushed to pick it up.

"Hello?"

"Hey baby, what you doing?" Wesley asked.

"Just sitting here thinking about you, why?"

"Just wondering, that's all."

"Oh, is that right?" She replied smiling. "Well, what time will you be home?"

"About six o'clock, why?"

"Just wondering," she said mocking him.

"Now you wanna be funny, huh?"

"Nah, I was asking 'cause I got a surprise for you when you get home."

"Oh yeah, and what might that be?"

"If I told you, it wouldn't be a surprise, now would it?"

"Ok, you're right, but could you at least give me a hint?"

"Let's just say I want us to get in some more practice trying new things."

"Ooh, I like the way that sounds already."

"Yeah, well you need to hurry up and get here 'cause I'm ready to get started."

"Damn, it's like that?"

"Ever since the other night, it's been like that."

"Why haven't you said anything?"

"Because you seemed preoccupied with other things. Besides, I had to get my mind right."

"Wait a minute!" Wesley replied, "What you mean you had to get your mind right?"

"Well, you know, all of this is sort of new to me and I kind of enjoyed how things went."

"Oh, is that right?" Wesley said with a smirk.

"Yeah, I've been practicing and I think I'm ready now.

"Practicing! Now you've really lost me."

"Wesley, just get here and all your questions will be answered."

"But..."

"Oh yeah," she said cutting him off. "And I'm laying here waiting naked."

"Damn! In that case give me thirty minutes."

***

Spoon sat on the edge of the bed counting the money they'd made so far. Two thousand dollars wasn't bad for half a day's work. With Clarence sitting in the living room watching TV, they waited for Germ to get back because there was definitely more money to be made.

Stacking the money by denominations, he placed rubber bands around each pile before placing the money in the bag he had in the closet. Removing another two ounces, he closed the bag and lay back on the bed next to Sonya. She lay on her back wearing nothing but a pair of boy shorts and a wife beater, practically leaving nothing to the imagination and while lying there, all she could think about was how he'd made her feel earlier.

Rolling over on her stomach, she kissed his neck while massaging his dick through his pants. Then reaching for his zipper, she unzipped his pants and pulled him free.

"Damn!" She thought to herself while massaging him back and forth. Spoon had definitely changed and without another word, she slid down the bed and took him in her mouth. Spoon gasped as her warm mouth engulfed him and giving into her, he watched as she took him deep into her throat. Sonya couldn't believe how big he'd gotten since the last time they were together and wondered what it would feel like to have him inside of her. She knew that eventually

she'd find out, but right now her focus was on the task at hand.

Grabbing the base of his dick, she begin deep throating him over and over again as he ran his fingers through her hair. Then while looking up at him seductively, she released him. "I want to feel you inside of me," she said before sliding off the bed and removing her shirt and panties. Them climbing back on the bed, she squatted over him. Reaching back to grab his dick, she placed him at her opening and after planting her hands firmly on his chest, she lowered herself down onto him. "Mmm," she moaned softly and as he reached around to caress her ass, she began riding him.

Spoon loved the way her pussy gripped him as she slid up and down his length, and while tightly gripping her ass, he pushed up into her with every stroke. Continuously she rode him, loving the way he filled her up, as Spoon reached up to caress her tits. Sonya was in heaven as he drove his dick deeper inside of her and she rode him like there was no tomorrow. Continuing to grind her hips back and forth into him, she kissed him passionately, then suddenly catching him off guard she climbed off of him, knelt between his legs and took him back in her mouth. Spoon couldn't believe how much she'd grown as he watched her take him in and out of her mouth. But one thing he was certain of, she definitely wasn't the same little girl from high school. For the next ten minutes, Sonya licked, sucked, and massaged his dick and when he came, she swallowed all he had to give.

Climbing up to lay down next to him, Sonya turned to kiss him passionately and seconds later he came up for air.

"You got anybody coming over here to see you?'

"Somebody like who?"

"You know, like a boyfriend or something?"

"I got friends but ain't nothing serious. Why?"

"'Cause I want you to call 'em and let 'em know that you got a man now."

"Spoon, don't be playing, alright? We too old to be 'bout that bullshit."

"Who said I was playing?" Spoon replied with a smile.

"Alright, but remember you said it."

"What, you don't want me as your man?"

"I ain't saying that."

"So what are you saying?"

"Nothing. I mean, I wouldn't mind. I just don't need no unnecessary drama. You know how y'all niggas get when y'all start getting a little money."

"You ain't gotta worry about that," Spoon replied. "'Cause like I told you earlier, as long as you stay straight with me, I got you."

"Alright now Spoon, don't let me catch none of those hoes in your face."

"Nah, that's your spot and you better represent it to the fullest."

"Oh, don't worry," she said smiling.

"Alright, but I need to ask you something."

"What?"

"Who lives in apartment two twenty six?"

"Oh, that's Old Man Harry, but why you asking 'bout him?"

"'Cause I need to know who he is."

"Put it like this, he's somebody you don't want to be fucked up with."

"Hold up! You act like I'm soft or something."

"Nah I ain't saying that, but Old Man Harry don't play."

"Shit, I'm the ma'fucka who don't play," Spoon declared.

"Yeah I hear you, but you ever heard of somebody named Hood?"

"Growing up. Why?"

"Well, that's who Old Man Harry works for and trust me, they might be kind of old, but them ma'fuckers don't care about nobody. I remember one time, somebody shot one of them, and the police had the person who shot him in the back of the police car. One of the old ma'fuckers drove up, got out of his car with a gun and shot the dude through the window of the damn police car."

"What did the police do after he did that?"

"They shot him, but I'm saying who the fuck gon' walk up and shoot somebody sitting in the back of a police car besides somebody who's crazy?"

"Well, what about this nigga Hood I hear everybody talking 'bout?"

"I don't really know about him, but from what I hear, he's the worse one. Why you asking about them?"

"Oh, I just wanted to know who they was."

"Spoon listen, don't be fucked up with them old ma'fuckas."

"Nah, they better not be fucked up with me," Spoon replied while climbing out of bed. As he buckled his pants, Sonya just shook her head because she knew he wouldn't listen. "I want some more of that later," he said while gazing down at her.

"I ain't going nowhere," she shot back. "And you can get it when you want it."

"I'm feelin' that," he said before walking out the room and noticing Germ, he smiled.

"So what's up, you got that?"

"Yeah," Germ replied before handing him one of the guns.

"Alright then, let's go get this money."

***

Walking into the apartment, Wesley noticed Carla laying on the couch naked with a smile on her face. While approaching her, she looked up at him.

"What took you so long?"

"I got here as fast as I could," he replied while beginning to undress, and suddenly sitting up, she helped him. With his pants down around his ankles, Wesley looked on as she removed something from a bag behind the couch and sprayed it on his dick.

"Something new, I see," he said smiling.

"It's what you wanted, right?"

"Well, yeah…"

"Ok then, let the games begin."

CHAPTER 14

Standing in his kitchen cooking up the work he'd gotten from Wesley, Moose couldn't shake the feeling that he somehow knew the young cat that almost bumped into him in the hallway of the Carol City Apartments. He remembered the alarming look on his face, as though he was caught doing something he wasn't supposed to. At the time he didn't think much of it, but while lying in bed last night he replayed the scene over in his mind and could see the young man's face clear as day. *"Oh well,"* he thought, *"I'll figure it out eventually."* Until then, he had other things to concentrate on. Setting the work out to dry, his thoughts drifted back to the two young cats that were trying to sell the two keys and he realized that he couldn't suspect everybody trying to sell work. Regardless of what, somebody took it and before it was all over, they'd find out who.

***

Already late for work, Wesley sat in traffic exhausted from a night of lovemaking with Carla. He was amazed at the things she was now willing to try, but what surprised him the most was when she deep throated him. She explained to him how she'd practiced for two days using a porno tape and dildo given to her by her friend Sheila. Then, if that wasn't enough, they watched the tape together. Now pulling up to his workplace, he parked, got out, and headed inside where he was met by his secretary.

"Good morning, Mr. Wesley, I'm glad you're here. The boss is in the conference room with the County Commissioner and the people from the Evergreen Corporation."

"What's he doing in there?" Wesley asked surprisingly.

"Don't you remember? You had an eight o'clock for the new American Airlines Arena."

"Oh, shit! I totally forgot," Wesley replied.

"Well the boss has been looking for you and he's pissed, so I suggest you go on up."

"Alright, and thanks Claire," he said before heading for the stairs and while rushing up, he chastised himself for forgetting something so important.

Finally reaching the conference room door, Wesley straightened himself up, stuck out his chest, and walked in. Everyone got quiet and his boss glared at him as he took his seat.

"I apologize for being late, but it was unavoidable. Now could someone please bring me up to speed on what I've missed so far?"

"Glad you could make it," his boss said sarcastically. "I was just telling these fine gentleman that this land deal will not only be good for our city, but it could be very lucrative for them as well."

"Ok," Wesley replied as he stood and opened his briefcase. Then after removing several files, he walked around the conference room while handing one to each person present.

"Gentleman, if you'd please follow along, I'm going to show you why purchasing the land can be a great investment. First, if you would turn to page one, you will notice that according to the land survey I've prepared, this parcel of land sits directly in the heart of downtown Miami, making it accessible by car, boat, and air. As you all know, this is the proposed site of the new American Airlines Arena, which will be home to the Miami Heat franchise. It can also be used to host other venues such as concerts, the music awards, and business symposiums. Gentleman, your investment will be retuned tenfold in as little as ten years should you agree to the current asking price."

"Mr. Wesley, my name is Mr. Wellington and I'm the lawyer representing the Evergreen Corporation. Now, while I'm impressed with your presentation, my problem is with your asking price of twenty million dollars."

"Well Mr. Wellington, while twenty million dollars may sound substantial, it's a fair price for such a lucrative return. You see, given the proximity of this land, it's considered prime real estate and not only is it worth the price, I'm sure we could get more. Seated at the table with you is the County Commissioner, Bob Mitchell, who can guarantee that the city would be willing to lease this land from your client for the next twenty years at say two million dollars a year, giving your client forty million by the time the lease expires. We'll even throw in season tickets to the Heat games."

"That's very tempting," Mr. Wellington replied with a smile, "but what other assurances can my client receive that will show him that he's not just pissing his money in the wind?"

"Oh, I can assure you Mr. Wellington that your client will not be pissing his money in the wind. This project is worth six hundred million dollars with the team's owner contributing three hundred million, the county of Miami-Dade contributing two hundred million, and taxpayers footing the rest of the bill. So you see, regardless if you purchase this land or not, the new arena will be built right on this very spot and whoever owns the land is going to get filthy rich."

"Well in that case, why doesn't the county keep it and profit off of it themselves?"

"First of all, I'm sure you're familiar with land taxes, am I correct?"

"Most certainly, what businessman isn't?"

"Well then, I'm sure that you're also aware the large tax bill that Miami Dade County taxpayers are saddled with each year due to undeveloped properties such as this."

"What does that have to do with anything?"

"The sale of this property will eliminate some of that burden."

"Yes, and saddle the purchaser of the property with it. Isn't that correct, Mr. Wesley?"

"Well if you want to call a twenty million dollar profit a burden, then yes Mr. Wellington, you're correct," Wesley replied while glaring at Mr. Wellington with contempt.

"Gentleman," Wesley's boss suddenly said, breaking the tension. "What do you say we take a thirty minute break to think about what's been discussed?"

"I think it's a splendid idea," Mr. Wellington replied. "Besides, it'll give me some time to consult with my client on a few matters."

"Mr. Commissioner, what do you think?"

"Well, I think it'll give us all time to simmer down a bit and look at this from different angles."

"Personally, I think it's a bunch of bullshit on Mr. Wellington's part," Wesley suddenly replied, shocking everyone in the room. "You see Mr. Wellington, I also know that you have a more personal stake in this deal than you've led on."

"Why, that's ridiculous," Mr. Wellington screamed. "What would make you say such a thing?"

"For one, because I know a few of the wealthy people you represent besides the Evergreen Corporation and I know that a few of them would be glad to purchase this land for the reasons I stated earlier. Now, whatever your motive is for not wanting the Evergreen Corporation to buy this land, I'm not sure it's not in the best interest of your client sitting beside you, but rather yours."

"I will not sit here and listen to your unfounded allegations, because I have always worked in the best interest of my client."

"Is that so?" Wesley responded sarcastically while removing another sheet of paper from his briefcase, then handing it to Mr. Evergreen, he turned to face Mr. Wellington, "Well would you care to explain why you're being investigated for undermining the interests of a few of your former clients? Mr. Evergreen, you've heard my proposals and you've seen the projections for yourself. As of now, the offer still stands and I'm certain we can get this deal done without Mr. Wellington. Besides, if we can, you'll be saving yourself the two percent fee he would've been paid."

"Young man, you're right," Mr. Evergreen replied. "I've suspected you for some time but now that I know for sure, you're fired."

"You can't fire me," Mr. Wellington screamed.

"I just did and if you go anywhere near the office, I'll have you arrested. Now if you'll excuse us, we have business to discuss."

As Mr. Wellington gathered his papers and walked out, Mr. Evergreen turned to Wesley.

"Young man, I agree to your terms and I'd also like to thank you for exposing Mr. Wellington for what he really is. As for the two percent fee, I'd like to give it to you for doing such an outstanding job."

"Mr. Evergreen, you don't have to do that, I'm just doing what I'm paid to do."

"Oh, but I insist. And speaking of doing what you're paid to do, if you ever decide to go private, give me a call 'cause I could use someone like you."

"I'll keep that in mind," Wesley replied with a smile.

"Now gentleman, if you'll excuse me, I have a plane to catch. Have your lawyers fax me the paperwork and I'll sign it and get it back to you as soon as possible. Have a good day, gentleman," was the last thing he said before walking out.

"Damn son, that was some of the best work I've seen in a long time," the Commissioner said patting Wesley on the back.

"Well sir, sometimes you have to outmaneuver your opponent," Wesley replied.

"Well, you certainly did that."

"Yeah, and almost gave me a damn heart attack," Wesley's boss added.

"You've gotta have faith, boss."

"Faith my ass, where did you get the dirt on Mr. Wellington?"

"If I told you, I'd have to kill you."

"Oh yeah? Well what about this two percent fee Mr. Evergreen just gave you?"

"You heard the man, he insisted."

"You didn't seem to put up much resistance."

"Well, it was either that or give you my letter of resignation and take the job he offered."

"Then I'd have to kill you," his boss replied as they all laughed.

"Well gentleman, I'm gonna get out of here so I can inform the County Board members that the deal's been finalized," the Commissioner said.

"Take care, Mr. Mitchell," Wesley replied and as the Commissioner walked out, Wesley turned to his boss. "I apologize for being late."

"Oh don't worry about it. I mean, I'll admit I was upset at first, but with the performance I just witnessed, how could I argue with you? Matter of fact, take the rest of the day off."

"Are you serious?"

"Yeah, 'cause you deserve it. Now go on, get out of here."

"In that case, thank you."

"Don't mention it, Wesley." And as he turned to leave, he said, "See you in the morning, and don't be late."

CHAPTER 15

Eyvette was having a bad day. In addition to having the sixteen-year-old in her courtroom for selling drugs, she also had two fourteen-year-olds, a twelve-year-old and an eleven-year-old who was arrested for having a loaded gun in school. Sitting in her office, she wondered where did the parents and society go wrong with these kids and why were so many of them getting caught up in the system? She also wondered about her own eighteen-year-old and although he wasn't really a bad child, she knew that peer pressure could lead even the best ones to go astray. Going over her paperwork, her thoughts drifted to Wesley and their meeting tonight. She hoped that somehow they'd be able to come up with some answers, because at the rate the young kids were getting themselves killed and locked up, soon they'd truly be the lost generation.

***

Wesley welcomed being able to get off early and although he would've loved to go home and sleep, he decided instead to go check on Moose. Pulling up in front of his friend's house, Wesley got out, walked to the door, and knocked. Seconds later, Moose opened the door and invited him in.

"So what's up?" He asked as Wesley entered.

"Just stopped by to see if you heard anything about the missing work?"

"Nah, not yet," Moose replied. "But I got a feeling that we're gonna hear something soon."

"What makes you say that?"

"'Cause whoever got it gon' have to try to get rid of it sooner or later. I just don't see some kids holding on to that much dope and not try to get no money off of it."

"I feel you, but if they know any better, they better not let me find out," Wesley replied.

"Just chill, 'cause they got to come out of hiding sooner or later."

"Yeah, you're right. What's up with the other shit?"

"Well, I got sixty thousand dollars from the first two and fifteen thousand so far off of what you gave me last night. I'll make my rounds later, so I should have more by morning."

"That's cool, but did you subtract the twenty grand I told you to keep for yourself?"

"Nah, I just added it in with the other money."

"Why? I told you to keep it for yourself."

"Well, I figured because somebody broke in and took four and a half keys, I'd give you the money to kind of make up for some of it, you feel me?"

"Nah nigga, I ain't feeling you," Wesley replied. "'Cause when I told you to keep it, it ain't had nothing to do with what them ma'fuckers took. Now, I understand that you feel responsible for them ma'fuckas coming in here, but let me ask you this. How long have you been keeping work in here?"

"For a while, why?"

"Just 'cause a ma'fucka break in it don't make it your fault. They could've broken into any one of the houses round here, it's just unfortunate that they chose yours. Don't sweat it though, 'cause like you said, sooner or later we'll hear something."

"Yeah, alright." Moose replied. "Now let me go get this money."

While Moose went to go get the money, Wesley thought about the loyalty he'd shown over the years and suddenly remembering the four hundred thousand dollars he'd made earlier, he decided to show his appreciation.

Seconds later, Moose came back carrying a bag of money and handed it to him. Reaching into the bag, Wesley removed fifteen thousand dollars and handed the bag back to him.

"What you want me to do with this?"

"Whatever you want, it's yours."

"Man, look…"

"Nah, you look," Wesley said, cutting him off. "You had seventy five thousand dollars in the bag, right?"

"Yeah."

"Alright, I got fifteen of it which I'm gon' give to Risco Park so they can buy some equipment for their little league football teams. That leaves sixty thousand dollars and I'm giving it to you. Now what are you getting ready to do?"

"I was gon' make my rounds to see if everybody was straight and collect whatever money they got."

"Alright, and since I ain't got nothing to do until later, I'm gon' ride with you."

"I ain't got no problem with that but I know ma'fuckas gon' be surprised to see you."

"Good, and they might as well get used to it," Wesley replied.

"Well give me a minute and I'll be ready to go."

"Yeah, alright," Wesley shot back and after several minutes, they both got into Moose's truck and left to go make the rounds.

***

"Damn man, we done got rid of all that shit already?" Germ screamed.

"Hell yeah," Spoon replied. "You think we playin'?"

"Shit! We keep getting rid of this shit like this, we gon' be paid in no time."

"Damn right, but y'all check it. Clarence, I need for you to go home, get the other quarter, and have your cousin cook it up. Me and Germ gon' finish getting rid of this last ounce, then we'll come by there."

"Alright, but what you want me to tell him when he asks about his money?"

"Tell him I'll be by there before he finishes and I got him. Matter of fact, I'm gon' bring another quarter with me and I might have him cook that up, too. Anyway, go handle that and we'll be by there in about an hour."

"Alright, I'll holla at y'all later," Clarence replied, and after walking off, Spoon and Germ got back to work.

"So when we gon' get paid?" Germ suddenly asked.

"I told y'all that I was gon' give y'all two grand off every quarter, right?"

"Yeah."

"Well I might have to change it to a grand, 'cause remember we're splitting all expenses three ways. And we got to put money up to re-up with."

"I feel you 'bout the expenses, but damn, a nigga can't get more than a grand?"

"Man listen, ma'fuckas don't get a grand a week, but I'm giving it to y'all off every quarter. Now who else you know gon' do that?"

"Nobody, but we supposed to be homeboys."

"Well if that's the case, you should know I got you. Y'all gotta let this shit get crunked up first, then we can stunt, you feel me?"

"Alright," Germ said and before he could say another word, he looked up to see Moose and Wesley coming down the hall. "Oh shit!" he screamed.

"What?" Spoon replied.

"That's the old man right there."

"What old man?"

"The old man whose house we broke in, who you think?"

"Damn, it sure is and that's the ma'fucka who was driving the Jag. Man, what they doin' round here?"

"I told you I saw 'em coming out of apartment two twenty six the other day."

"Yeah, I remember you telling me. You think they up to something?"

"I don't know, but that shit got me paranoid."

"Paranoid my ass, they coming 'round here for something."

"Yeah, they be hollarin' at the old ma'fucka in apartment two twenty six."

"I hear you, but why they looking this way?"

Germ looked up to see Moose looking in their direction and for a brief second, they made eye contact before Moose disappeared inside the apartment.

"Man, you saw that?"

"Yeah," Spoon replied. "And I don't know what's on in his mind, but if he come at a nigga with that bullshit, he can get it put on his ass."

***

"What's up?" their friend asked as they entered the apartment and took a seat.

"Ain't nothing, old timer," Wesley replied. "Just thought I'd come by and holla at you for a minute."

"It's been a long time since you've been out and about, ain't it?"

"Yeah, you can say that."

"What, hanging 'round all those politicians got so you don't wanna hang with common folks no more?"

"Now you know better than that, it's just that me doing what I'm doing is one of the main reasons we've lasted this long."

"Yeah, but you can at least show your face from time to time, don't you think?"

"Yeah, you're right, but don't worry 'cause you'll be seeing more of me from now on."

"Why, is something wrong?"

"No, but I know that you heard about somebody breaking into Moose's house and stealing some work."

"Yeah I heard about that and whoever it was must have a death wish."

"Well, I think it's time for Hood to put in a little work just to show ma'fuckas that shit ain't changed."

"Think they ready for that? Shit! The last bit of excitement we had was when Old Man Sam shot that young cat in the back of the police car for shooting Gus."

"Yeah, Sam was crazy, huh?"

"Nah, he wasn't crazy, he was just dead ass serious," the old timer replied.

"Yeah, but let me ask you something," Moose said. "Who are those young cats hanging out by the stairs?"

"I don't know, probably just some young niggas selling a little dope. Why?"

"Because one of 'em almost bumped into me the other day and for some reason, he acts like he knows me."

"You sure you ain't just trippin'?"

"Nah, 'cause today I caught him staring at me the same way."

"Man, you know how these young niggas are nowadays. Always think they gotta act hard."

"That's what happened to the young fella Todd, who used to be around here. He bought a lot of work from me, but he felt he had to disrespect people in order for them to respect him."

"What happened to him?"

"People got tired of it and put the man on him."

"Yeah, I hear you," Moose replied. "But I just got a funny feeling 'bout them young niggas."

"Well if it'll make you feel better, I'll keep an eye on 'em for you."

"I'll appreciate it."

"No problem, Moose. Now we gon' handle our business or we gon' sit here yakin' all day? 'Cause I'm getting a headache."

"Alright old timer, we'll finish our business and get gone," Wesley replied smiling.

Forty five minutes later, Moose and Wesley got up to leave and as they stepped outside, Moose looked down the hall towards the staircase. After seeing no one, they headed for his truck and while wondering where they'd gone, he had a funny feeling that they'd be seeing them again real soon.

CHAPTER 16

"Finally," Eyvette sighed. Her day had come to an end and now she had to rush home, take a shower, then meet Wesley for dinner at the Olive Garden. Smiling at the thought, she went downstairs, climbed into her Mercedes and headed home. Once there, she quickly undressed before jumping in the shower. Feeling refreshed as the water cascaded down her body, Eyvette once again thought of the young kids that came through her courtroom and knew that as a society, we were failing the younger generation.

Stepping out of the shower, she began drying off and smelled a faint odor which reminded her of something she couldn't quite put a finger on. Assuming her son and his friends were the cause, she made a mental note to talk to him later. But being pressed for time, she headed to her room to get dressed.

Dressed in a knee-length skirt and matching shirt, she complemented her outfit with a pair of three-inch heels and while looking at herself in the mirror, all she could say was, "Damn! I look good." After spraying on a touch of Chanel perfume, she grabbed her purse and car keys, then walking outside to her car she climbed in, pooped in a Keisha Cole CD, and drove to meet Wesley.

***

Arriving early to the restaurant, Wesley was led to his table and after ordering a bottle of wine, he waited for Ms. Summers to arrive. He didn't have to wait long, as he looked up to see her coming in dressed in her matching skirt and shirt which showed her curves. As she approached the table, he went around to pull out her chair as she took her seat.

"Thank you, Mr. Wesley."

"It's a pleasure and you look lovely," Wesley replied.

"Well, I'm glad I look better than I feel."

"Rough day, huh?"

"Rough ain't the word. Do you know that I had an eleven-year-old in my courtroom today for bringing a gun to school?"

"Are you serious?"

"Very, and I'd like to know where he got it from."

"Well, you know kids are growing up so fast nowadays and with both parents having to work, the kids are practically raising themselves."

"Well, the parents need to try something different, because this is getting ridiculous."

"I agree one hundred percent."

"Oh, Mr. Wesley, I'm so sorry," Eyvette suddenly said, "I'm so busy running my mouth, I didn't even ask how your day was."

"That's ok, I mean, it was just a normal day filled with board meetings. Nothing to write home about."

"Well, I apologize again and if I may add, you look handsome."

"Thank you, Ms. Summers," and before he could say another word, the waitress was standing at their table.

"Good evening, I'll be your waitress tonight. Would you like to place your order?"

"Yes please," Eyvette replied. "I'll have the Chicken Caesar Salad with ranch dressing."

"Ok, and you sir?"

"I'd like the steak and alfredo dinner with a side order of mixed vegetables."

"How would you like your steak, sir?"

"Medium rare, and can I have some A-1 Steak Sauce, please?"

"Sure, and what will you two be drinking?"

"Well, we already have a bottle of wine so that'll be fine."

"Ok, I'll be about fifteen minutes and if you have any more requests, just let me know

"Ok, and thank you," Eyvette said and as the waitress walked off, she turned her attention back to Wesley.

"As I was saying, these kids today are something else. I mean, the stuff they're doing, I couldn't even think about when I was young. My mother would have beat my behind."

"That's just it," Wesley replied. "We've gotten away from the traditional values taught to us by our parents and grandparents. Today's kids are given too many choices. I mean, you can't even spank your child without worrying about being put in jail."

"Yeah, but the police are instead killing them and locking them up."

"Well, it starts by teaching them the importance of education, because without it, you're destined to fail. I read somewhere that there are three times as many blacks in prisons than in college, with Latino's not far behind. In order for us to truly end the incarceration culture, we have to take a look at the root of the problem. Why is it that more than half of all black men in America don't finish high school? Why did congress abolish Pell Grants for prisoners and virtually eliminated all three hundred and fifty incarceration college programs? Is it any coincidence that six out of seven black men who drop out of high school have spent time in jail by their mid-thirties? With unemployment on the rise, arrests for non-violent infractions and petty crimes are leaving families motherless, fatherless, and hopeless. We live in a world that promotes law, order and justice, yet our actions often times prove otherwise. Right now, our kids are frequently finding themselves incarcerated at an early age and let's not forget our women who are in fact the largest growing segment of the prison population. Eighty five percent of women are now serving time for non-violent crimes, with black women six times as likely to get jail than their white counterparts. It's a sad reality."

"Yeah, one I witness every day," Eyvette replied. "Young black men and women being caught up in the system."

"It's funny you should say that, Ms. Summers, because you too are a part of this very same system."

"Mr. Wesley, I have a job to do."

"Hold up! I'm not saying that you should quit your job, all I'm saying is—take your son for example. Let's just say he got caught with drugs or better yet a gun by you, what would you do?"

"As a mother, I would try to find out why he was doing whatever he was doing and see if I could find him some help."

"So you wouldn't turn him in?"

"My son? No."

"Why? That's your job, right?"

"Yeah, but I know what the system can do to a child and I wouldn't want to subject my child to that."

"But you will to someone else's child, right?"

"I don't fully understand what you're saying, Mr. Wesley."

"You're a prosecutor, right?"

"Yes, that is correct."

"And your job is to prosecute for various crimes, correct?"

"You can say that."

"Well, you just said that if you caught your own son doing something wrong, you would try to help him rather than see him caught up in the system. Yet every day, you recommend punishment for other people's kids."

"You know, I never thought of it like that Mr. Wesley, I mean…"

"No need to explain Ms. Summers, 'cause you see, you're not alone. We as a society have become quick to condemn a child that's not our own, yet we will make excuses for our own when they mess up. If people would look at all kids as their own, they would start to do more to help them rather than condemn them, because all they lack is guidance. Well, most of them anyway."

Before she had a chance to respond, their dinner was served and each resigned to their thoughts as they ate in silence.

"Mmm! That was delicious," Eyvette said twenty minutes later while pushing her plate away.

"Yeah, and I didn't realize I was so hungry," Wesley replied.

"You know, while we were eating, I thought about what you said and you were right."

"On what account?"

"When you said that if people looked at all kids as their own instead of someone else's, people would start to do more to help them rather than condemning them. My question is, how do we help them?"

"First, we help build their self-esteem, 'cause a person with low self-esteem tends to use material possessions to define their self-worth."

"Like a young girl in search of love becoming promiscuous?" Eyvette replied.

"Exactly. But you see Ms. Summers, we must teach our kids what it means to be rich and I'm not talking about having millions of dollars. To me, being rich means being aware of the great wealth and value that a person possesses naturally with or without material gain. It means recognizing your talents and putting them to work in order to attain what you heart desires. We have to ask them question like, how well do you know yourself? Are you on the right path? What are your values? Because your values are what you deem worthwhile or desirable. This is the key to a person's value system. These factors will drive a person to his or her purpose in life and if they have no value system, then how can they be passionate about anything?"

"Do you have kids, Mr. Wesley?"

"Unfortunately no, but why do you ask?"

"Because you seem so passionate about helping kids, how did you learn all this stuff? Didn't you say you worked for a brokerage firm?"

"Yes I do, but before that I had my share of troubles and I've even spent time in prison."

"Are you serious? 'Cause I wouldn't have ever guessed."

"Yeah, well it took that for me to realize that there was a better life and by using my experience, if I can keep one child from having to go through what I went through, then what I'm doing is worth it."

"I just wish there were more men like you willing to step up to the plate and give the younger generation more to look forward to."

"Now, I'm no saint Ms. Summers, not by a longshot, but what I'm hoping to show the younger generation is that you can have the life you want if you just educate yourself and apply what you've learned."

"Well, I'm sure a lot of them look up to you. And who knows, maybe you can keep more than one of them out of jail."

"I hope so, 'cause God knows we've lost enough of them already."

"Amen to that," she replied smiling. "You know, I'm glad that we had the chance to talk, Mr. Wesley. And if it's ok with you, I'd very much like to see you again."

"Oh really, now? As in… see me how?"

"To put it bluntly, I'd like to have another dinner date with you, if I'm not intruding."

"Oh no, and I'd love that. I truly enjoyed the conversation, and besides, I'd like to get to know you better."

"Good, then it's settled. How about I call you and let you know when and where?"

"I have an idea, how about I call you and let you know when I'll be picking you up?"

"Ooh! That's fine with me and I look forward to your call."

As Wesley went to pay the tab, Eyvette looked at him lustfully and thought *"Damn! What a man."* Then as they walked to their cars, he noticed her watching him out of the corner of her eye. After reaching her car, he hugged her goodnight before walking to his car, climbing behind the wheel, and heading home.

CHAPTER 17

"Wait a minute!" Clarence screamed. "This ain't but a thousand dollars. I thought you said we were getting two grand off every quarter?"

"Yeah I did," Spoon replied. "But like I told Germ, I had to change it up 'cause remember we're splitting everything three ways, plus we gotta put some money to the side so we can re-up."

"I hear you, but that wasn't the agreement."

"Clarence listen, most ma'fuckas ain't even getting a grand a week, y'all getting a grand off of every quarter. Shit! For every key we get rid of, y'all making four grand and if you think about it, once we get rid of what we got y'all will have eighteen thousand dollars and y'all ain't really have to do shit."

"Nigga you crazy, I'm stashing that shit here and we cooking that shit here. If my ole woman finds out, I'm the one who got to explain that shit."

"I feel you, but remember we the ones who brought you in on this shit in the first place. I ain't mean like a nigga need you, I mean me and Germ the ones who went in the house and found the shit, so if shit hits the fan it's on us, not you."

"Hold up, nigga! You know damn well if shit go down, I'm gon' have y'all backs so don't come at me like that."

"So stop complaining 'bout nothing and help me get this thang jumping so all us can eat."

"What you mean? I've been helping since day one."

"Look, what I'm talking 'bout is opening up shop on the other side of the apartments, too. I just need somebody reliable who can handle that."

"Ah nigga, I'll have that shit jumping in no time. When you want to get started?"

"Shit! Right now," Spoon screamed. "I brought another quarter with me and we can get your cousin to cook it. That way, we'll have the whole apartments on lock."

"Now that's what I'm talking 'bout," Germ said. "So what y'all need me to do?"

"Your job gon' be to make sure we always got work. We gon' keep the shit at Sonya's apartment so you won't have to go far to get it, plus you'll be collecting the money and dropping it off to her."

"Alright, but who y'all gon' get to help y'all get rid of the work?"

"Damn, I ain't think about that," Spoon replied. "Matter of fact, we gon' need at least two people who want to get some money."

"Let's swing by the park and holla at a few people."

"Alright, but we paying three hundred dollars a week to start, so whoever we holla at make sure you let 'em know up front."

"Yeah alright," Clarence replied. "But if we gon' cook the rest of this shit we need to hurry up, 'cause my ole woman will be home soon."

"Yeah, plus we need to get back over to the apartments 'cause ain't no tellin' how much money we've missed," Spoon added.

Pulling out the other quarter key, Spoon handed it to Shorty Fats who immediately got to work while the three of them waited. An hour later, they all headed to the park.

***

James and Rick still hadn't gotten rid of the two keys, and as they drove around they decided to stop by Scott Park.

"Man, I'm tired of riding 'round with this shit," James screamed.

"Yeah, well maybe we can find somebody here who'll buy it," Rick replied.

"I guess anything's worth a try right now as long as it ain't them old ma'fuckas we ran into the other day."

"Man, I still don't know what that was about, but whatever it was it ain't got nothing to do with us."

Finally arriving at the park, they parked the car, got out and started walking. Minutes later, James overheard Spoon talking to a few young cats.

"Listen, if y'all want to make some money, I'll start y'all off at three hundred dollars a week."

"Man, that's straight," one of the young men said. "But we go to school during the day and our old ladies ain't gon' let us be out all times of night."

"Damn!" Spoon thought to himself. "Alright, well look, if y'all change y'all mind, just holla at me."

"Yeah, alright." The young boys replied before walking off and as Spoon turned to leave, he spotted James approaching him.

"Hey man, I overheard you saying that if a nigga wanted to make some money, you'll pay three hundred dollars a week to start."

"Yeah, why? You want to put in some work?" Spoon asked while eyeing him warily.

"Nah not really, but I'm tryin' to sell some work."

"Well I ain't tryin' to buy nothin' right now, but what you got?"

"Man, I got two of them thangs and they're going for the low."

"What, two ounces?"

"Nah, I got two keys and all I want is fifteen apiece."

"Fifteen!"

"Yeah, a nigga just looking for a quick come up, you feel me?"

"Oh I feel you, but check this out. Me and two of my partners got this lil' trap and we tryin' to get it jumpin'. If you want, you can get down with us and get rid of your work, but we want two thousand and five hundred dollars off every quarter."

"Damn! Well how much you getting off a quarter?"

"Nine grand."

"Well, I'm gon' have to talk to my partner and see what he says."

"Shit, where he at? I'll holla at him myself 'cause we're looking for two people to get down with us anyway."

"He's round here somewhere," and as they looked around, Spoon spotted Germ talking to someone.

"There he is right there," James said pointing in their direction.

The two of them began walking over to where Rick and Germ stood talking when Germ suddenly looked up to see them heading his way.

"Hey, Spoon! I got somebody I want you to meet." He screamed.

"Alright, what's up?" Spoon replied.

"This my dog Rick, we was in juvenile hall together and guess what?"

"He's trying to sell two keys."

"Damn! How'd you know that?"

"'Cause this is his partner right here," Spoon said while pointing at James.

"I told him I'd holla at you, but since you already know—"

"Well Rick, like I was telling James, I ain't really trying to cop no work right now 'cause I'm just starting out myself. We got a lil' trap over in the Carol City Apartments and we're trying to have that shit on lock, you feel me? Now, y'all can get rid of y'all shit in the trap if y'all want 'cause we looking for two people to put in work anyway. James told me y'all tryin' to get fifteen stacks a piece for the two keys."

"Yeah, just a little come up, you feel me?"

"Well, I got a deal that will get y'all more money. Say the both of y'all get down with us and y'all get rid of the work in our trap. All we want is two thousand and five hundred dollars per quarter, which will leave y'all six thousand and five hundred dollars per quarter. If we do it like that, y'all will get twenty six thousand dollars per key, which is eleven thousand dollars more than y'all tryin' to get. Now, y'all say y'all got two keys, so that's fifty two thousand dollars instead of thirty."

"Now, that's what's up!" Rick screamed, "My dog Germ was tellin' me you was 'bout your business."

"So what's up, y'all want to get down or what?"

"That depends on my partner, you know we in this together."

"Shit, let's get this money." James replied.

"Alright then, it's settled," Spoon said. "Now y'all check it, y'all know where the Carol City Apartments at, right?"

"Yeah, why?"

"'Cause that's where we got our trap."

"Oh, shit!" James screamed.

"What?"

"Man, we was just over there the other day."

"Oh yeah?"

"Hell yeah, and a couple of old ma'fuckas said they were looking to buy some work, but when we got there they took us to an apartment and just looked at the shit before telling us to get out."

"Damn, and they didn't buy it?"

"Nah, the one named Moose is who looked at it and all he said was 'it ain't ours.'"

"What he meant by that?"

"I don't know and I really don't care," Rick said. "All I know is a nigga ready to get some money, and fifty two thousand dollars sounds damn good to me."

"Well, we're goin' over there now, what y'all gon' do, meet us over there?"

"Shit, y'all can ride with us if y'all want to," James replied.

"Alright, well let's go get this money," Spoon said, and as they all piled into James's car and left the park, Spoon thought about the old men. Then he thought about all the money they were gonna make, and his last thought was *"Fuck it!"*

CHAPTER 18

Walking into his apartment, Wesley got the surprise of his life as Carla met him at the door, pushed him up against it, and began unbuckling his pants.

"Damn!" He said smiling, "What did I do to receive this welcome?"

"Why would you have to do something for me to be happy to see you?"

"I don't, it's just that I'm not use to this."

"Well," she said while getting down on her knees and looking up at him, "get used to it, 'cause this is what you wanted from me, right?"

"Well, yeah, sort of."

"Then stop trippin' and relax," she shot back before taking him in her mouth.

Wesley threw his head back and closed his eyes as she began sucking him in and out of her mouth. He couldn't believe how good she'd gotten at giving head but he damn sure wasn't complaining. Meanwhile, Carla continued licking and sucking his dick, occasionally deep throating him as he moaned with pleasure. She'd grown confident of her oral skills and marveled at the way he responded when she performed. Then again, he was her man and it was her job to please him or, like Sheila had said, if she didn't, another woman surely will.

Continuously, she sucked him in and out of her throat as he ran his fingers through her hair. Then just as suddenly as she began, she stopped, stood up, and kissed him. "You liked that?" She asked smiling.

"Hell yeah, but why'd you stop?"

"'Cause I want us to do it to each other," she replied while grabbing his hand and leading him to the couch. Then pushing him backwards, she finished undressing him before climbing up and straddling him in the sixty-nine position. Wesley wasted no time burying his face between her legs as he began licking and sucking her pussy hungrily.

Carla couldn't believe that she'd deprived herself of so much pleasure for so long, but as her head bobbed up and down on his dick, she was determined to make up for lost time.

For the next twenty minutes, they devoured each other with abandon. Licking, sucking, slurping on each other as they both moaned with pleasure. Suddenly, Carla's body tensed as she pressed her pussy down into his mouth and came. Wesley welcomed her sweet nectar as he continued licking and sucking her forbidden fruit. Not to be outdone, Carla increased her pace and began deep throating him over and over again until he flooded her mouth with his juices. Finally climbing off of him, she smiled as she lay down beside him.

"Damn! You taste good," he said while taking her in his arms.

"Oh, yeah? Well, so do you," she replied while positioning herself on all fours. Then looking back at him she said the words he wanted to hear, "Now I want to feel you."

"Believe me you ain't gotta say it twice," he replied as he got behind her, grabbed her by her waist and entered her slowly. Once he was deep inside of her, he began sliding his dick in and out of her while pulling her into him.

Carla pushed back into him as he fucked her from behind, then reaching back between her legs she began massaging his balls as he continued to bury himself deep inside of her. Increasing the pace, Wesley fucked her hard and fast with long, deep strokes. As he felt himself about to come and unable to hold back any longer, he flooded her insides.

Carla road the wave of pleasure as she pushed back into him, gritted her teeth and moaned with pleasure. Pulling out of her, he lay down next to her.

"Damn! You're insatiable," he said while turning to face her.

"You made me like this and now you're complaining?"

"Nah, I ain't complaining, I'm just surprised at how comfortable you've gotten with me."

"Like I told you, when you're growing up and people are constantly telling you that only whores do this and that, after a while you start to believe it."

"Well you ain't no whore, you're my woman."

"I know that, but I want to make you happy."

"Oh, you definitely do that, but where did you come up with the idea to meet me at the door when I got home?"

"I saw it on a tape I got from Sheila. Why, you liked that?"

"Hell yeah, but what else have you learned from watching those tapes?"

"How about I just show you," she replied smiling and without another word, she climbed on top of him.

***

Back at Eyvette's house, she was walking through the door when she smelled that same odor again. "What is that smell?" She said to herself as she rushed to open the windows. Moving from room to room, she could still smell the faint odor and it upset her. "I done told that boy about having his friends all up in my house while I'm not here," she mumbled, "but his hardheaded behind just won't listen. I work too hard to have people messing up my stuff, just wait till he gets home."

Still mumbling to herself, she walked into his room and found his things scattered everywhere and while heading for his window, something caught her attention. Turning suddenly towards the closet, she spotted the green duffel bag and wondered where her son had gotten it. With no job, he couldn't afford to buy it and she hadn't bought it for him, so where did it come from?

Reaching down to pick it up, she set it on the bed, then nervously she unzipped it. Looking inside, she noticed another bag containing a white substance and being a prosecutor for so many years, she knew that she was looking at a bag of cocaine.

"Oh God, no!" She said to herself as she sat on the edge of the bed staring at the bag she held in her hands. Why did her son have drugs in his room? And what was he doing with it? A million questions ran through her mind, then shock turned to anger as she placed it back in the duffel bag and began searching his room.

She'd done everything she could to raise him the right way and because he was eighteen, she tried respecting his privacy. *"No more,"* she thought to herself while tearing through his room like a bat out of hell, and thirty minutes later her efforts payed off when she found one thousand and five hundred dollars stashed in one of his shoes. Staring at the money, the reality that her son was selling drugs hit her. But why? Hadn't she provided everything he needed? Or had she failed him as a parent like so many others? One thing was certain, they'd talk when he got home. He was her son, her only child, and she wasn't about to lose him. Throwing the money in the bag, she snatched it up and headed for her room to wait for him to come home. He definitely had some explaining to do.

***

With her back to him, Carla rode Wesley as he looked on in surprise. With every stroke, he pushed his dick deeper inside of her while squeezing her ass gently. It amazed him what their little talk had done for their sex life. And if he'd known it would turn out this good, he'd have put his foot down sooner.

Climbing off of him, Carla laid on her back and spread her legs as Wesley positioned himself between them. Then pushing her legs back farther, he entered her and began sliding his dick back and forth. *"It gets no better than this,"* Carla thought to herself as she lay there looking up at Wesley. *"And who'd have ever thought that good dick could make a woman feel this good?"*

Looking down at her, Wesley knew that she'd do anything for him and it was evident by her opening up sexually in spite of what she was raised to believe. While watching his dick disappear inside of her repeatedly, he was determined not to disappoint her. Pulling in and out of her, he motioned for her to lay on her side and as she complied, he positioned one of her legs between his, grabbed her other leg and held it high above his head. Then grabbing his dick, he slid it inside of her and began fucking her with long deep strokes. Carla loved the way he felt inside of her and with this position, he left no room to spare. Although he'd said she pleased him and made him happy, she was determined to make sure.

Sensing that he was about to come, she pushed him onto his back, got up on her knees in front of him, and took him in her mouth, deep throating him over and over again. "Damn!" Wesley said to himself as he watched her head bob up and down on his dick and without warning, he came. Carla didn't miss a beat as she swallowed every drop and still licking and sucking him in and out of her warm mouth, she was determined to pleasure him.

"Damn! That was a hell of a welcome home."

"I'm glad you liked it," she replied while snuggled close to him.

"Like it? I loved it. I mean, it's not as bad as you initially thought, now is it?"

"No, and it's like the more we do it, the more I want it. Is that bad?"

"Nah, it ain't bad."

"I'm glad, 'cause I like pleasing you."

"I like pleasing you, too," he replied. "But I also plan to keep it interesting."

"Oh yeah? And just how do you plan to do that?"

"Well, I thought we could see which one of us can come up with the best surprise."

"Ok, and what does the winner get?"

"Whatever their heart desires…?"

"Alright, you're on," she said, "But I'm warning you, if I win, I want a ring on my finger."

"Ok, but it had better be good."

"Oh, trust me, it will be," she replied as she laid her head on his chest, and as she dozed off to sleep she thought about how she was going to pull it off.

CHAPTER 19

"Where are you coming from this time of the morning?" Eyvette asked as her son walked in the door.

"Out with my friends," Clarence replied.

"Do you realize that it's three in the morning?"

"Ah ma, nothing happened. Besides, I'm eighteen."

"I don't care, the only people running the streets this time of morning are cops and robbers and the last time I checked, you wasn't a cop."

"Well don't worry, 'cause I wasn't out robbing."

"So, what were you doing?"

"Just hanging out with my friends."

"Where?"

"Why the questions all of a sudden?"

"Because I'm your mother, and I want to know what my son is doing out in the streets at three in the morning."

"Like I told you, I was just hanging out with a few of my friends."

"Hanging out doing what, Clarence?"

"Doing nothing ma. Why are you trippin'?"

"Oh, you wanna know why I'm tripping? Because I've been in your room, and you know what I found?"

Clarence stood silent as the reality of what she said hit him.

"Oh, you can't talk now, huh? Well I'll tell you what I found, Mr. I'm Eighteen. I found a duffle bag with drugs in it. Now you want to tell me what it's doing in my house?"

"You have no right to go in my room and search through my things." Clarence replied in an attempt to shift the blame, but Eyvette wasn't having it.

"Let me tell you something," she said moving within inches of him. "First of all, this is my house, you just live here and until you get your own, that's how it's gonna be. Second, how could you be so stupid, Clarence? I work hard to keep a roof over your head, food on the table, and clothes on your back and this is how you thank me by bringing drugs in my house?"

"Mama I'm sorry, but I was just holding it for somebody."

"Holding it for somebody! Do you realize what would happen if somebody else would've found it? Not only would you be going to jail, but I could lose my job. Every day, I see boys your age and younger coming in my courtroom with drug charges, gun charges, and in some cases, even murder charges. Now you let me tell you something, I will not stand and watch you throw your life away running the streets with your so-called friends. So, from now on, they're not welcome in this house, do you understand me?"

"Yeah, I hear you."

"What did you say?"

"I said yes ma'am, I understand you."

"That's what I thought you said, and where'd you get the one thousand and five hundred dollars I found in your shoe?"

"I was holding that for my friend, too."

"Well if he wants it back, tell him he'll have to see me."

"Ah ma, why you got to go there?"

"Because I want to meet the person who got my son stashing drugs in my house."

"You ain't gotta worry 'bout it 'cause I'm giving it back to him in the morning."

"I don't know how you're gonna do that, 'cause I flushed it down the toilet."

"You did what?!" Clarence screamed.

"I flushed it down the toilet."

"Do you know how much that stuff costs?"

"No, and I don't care. Now do you know how much time you can get if you get caught with it?"

"I'm not gon' get caught."

"Yeah, that's what half the people sitting in prison said."

"Mom, do you realize what you've done? How am I gon' explain to my friend that my mom flushed his stuff down the toilet?"

"Honestly, I don't care what you tell him but I don't want him or anyone of your friends in my house again. Oh, and you, mister, are not allowed out of this house after twelve."

"Mom, I'm eighteen now, you can't treat me like a child anymore."

"When you start acting like a responsible adult, I'll treat you like one. Oh, and another thing, when I got home I smelled a funny odor. You wouldn't happen to know anything about that, would you?"

"Why would I know anything about that?"

"I was hoping you could tell me," Eyvette replied while still eyeing her son.

"Well, I don't know."

"Ok, I'll let you have that, but let me explain something to you. I can't tell somebody else how to raise their child, but Clarence, you're all I got and I'm not gonna lose you to the streets."

"But mom—"

"Hush, and let me finish. There are too many black men filling up the jails and prisons, and many others who never make it past the age of twenty. But if I can help it, you won't be one of them. Now, it's late and both of us can use some rest, so go to bed and we'll talk about it tomorrow."

As Clarence went to his room and closed the door, he didn't know what he was going to tell Spoon or how he was going to react to the news that his mother had flushed a quarter key of cocaine down the toilet. Getting undressed, he climbed into bed and as he laid there staring at the ceiling, the last thing he heard before dozing off to sleep was the sound of his mother crying.

***

Harry kept an eye for the young cats that were hanging out by the stairs. They'd come back accompanied by two other men after Moose and Wesley had left and he soon realized that they were the same ones who, days before, were trying to sell the two keys. When Moose had first mentioned them, he had no reason to suspect them of anything other than kids just trying to sell a little dope. Throughout the evening he watched them, and the assumptions proved right. They were selling dope under the stairs but they'd also branched out to the other side of the apartments. He was sure that Moose would love to know that. All night, people came and went buying dope from them. He also noticed one of them going in and out of the apartment where that crazy girl lived. Now sitting in his bedroom window watching them, he had the feeling that things were about to change around here, and not for the good. *"Oh well,"* he thought, *"this wasn't the first-time youngsters had come around and opened up shop and it probably wouldn't be the last. One thing was for sure, if they got besides themselves they'd get dealt with."*

CHAPTER 20

Walking into his office early the next morning, Wesley was summoned into his boss's office.

"What's up?" He asked after entering unannounced.

"Sit down Wesley, I need to talk to you."

"Why, is there something wrong?"

"No, not exactly, but it seems that Mr. Wellington has filed a complaint against you for the fiasco you pulled during our meeting with the Evergreen Corporation."

"You've got to be kidding me," Wesley replied.

"I wish I were, but unfortunately I got the call this morning."

"That little piece of shit is just mad that I exposed him for what he is."

"That may be true, but he tried collecting his bonus and was told that because of the allegation you logged against him, he's not entitled to it."

"So, what, he blames me?"

"It appears so, but that's not what I wanted to talk to you about."

"Alright then, what did you want to talk about?"

"First of all, Mr. Wellington is making a big stink about this and as a brokerage firm, we don't need bad PR.

"So, what are you saying?"

"I'm not saying anything other than if we were investigated, I'm afraid of what they'll find."

"Hold up! What do you mean you're afraid of what they'll find?"

"Well, remember there are a few controversial deals you've been involved in."

"Oh, I get it. After all the money I've brought in, the company wants to sacrifice me."

"No, nobody wants to sacrifice anybody. I'm merely suggesting that you take some time off until this blows over."

"In other words, you want me out of the way."

"Wesley, listen…"

"No, you listen. He's not the first person to file a complaint against me or this firm. What's so different now?"

"Well according to the complaint, he's accused you of using strong armed tactics to ensure deals, and here's the kicker. He's accusing you and the firm of running a kickback scheme."

"That's bullshit and you know it!" Wesley screamed.

"Yeah, but the firm doesn't need an audit team going through its books, because then a lot of the larger corporations won't want to be associated with us for fear of being pulled into the investigation."

"So in other words, I go on vacation so it appears like I'm being reprimanded by the firm. Then, the firm agrees to a settlement and everything's swept under the rug nice and neat."

"Something like that." His boss replied.

"You know," Wesley said while standing, "I came to work for this firm because it allowed me the freedom to be who I am. I've made a substantial amount of money for this firm, not including stock options. Then, there's the three million some odd dollars I've made you."

"Yes, you have, but you're missing the point."

"Am I really? The point is when things start to look a little shady, it's every man for himself and right now it seems like I'm the odd man out."

"Wesley, it's not like you're being let go. Look at it as an early vacation."

"I don't want a fucking vacation, can't you understand that? I want to do what I do and that's making deals."

"And you will, just after this situation blows over."

"You know, I've got a mind to call Mr. Evergreen about the job he offered me," Wesley said.

"Hold on now, don't go talking crazy," he boss replied. "All I'm asking is that you take a little time off to let things cool down around here. Then when you get back, it'll be business as usual."

"Yeah well, while I'm on vacation, I'm gonna have to think about whether or not I want to come back."

"Now Wesley…"

"'Now Wesley' my ass. For the last five years I've busted my ass for this company and now because some crooked ma'fucka files a complaint, you want me to tuck my tail and run."

"Now Wesley, I understand how you feel, but sometimes in life you lose by fighting even if you're right."

"Yeah, well that philosophy stinks because sometimes it's worth it to stand your ground, regardless of the outcome."

"You know you're right, but the fact remains that this is one battle the firm would rather not fight. So, like I said, take some time off until this blows over. I mean, it's not like you're hurting financially and when you come back, there will still be money to be made."

"Ok, as much as I don't want to do it, I will under one condition."

"Which is?"

"The Dana Corporation deal is mine and nobody messes with it but me."

"Fair enough and I'll keep you informed of any new development."

As Wesley started to leave, his boss looked up at him and said, "Thank you for understanding."

"Yeah, whatever," Wesley replied before walking out and closing the door behind him.

***

Eyvette sat at her desk going over her day's caseload, but she couldn't concentrate because her mind was on her son and the drugs she'd found in his room. When she'd left the house he was still asleep, so she decided they'd talk when she got home. What weighed heavily on her mind was the fact that while she sat at her desk, downstairs in the trunk of her car was a bag full of drugs and she had no idea what to do with it.

Last night, she was unable to sleep and after shedding a few tears, she laid in bed thinking about where she'd gone wrong as a parent and mother to her son. She had a successful career, kept food on the table, and made sure her son had everything a child could want. So then why would he choose to sell drugs? There were a lot of unanswered questions, but first she needed to figure out what to do with the drugs. Suddenly remembering her conversation with Mr. Wesley, she wondered if he'd understand, with no kids of his own, how Clarance could do this. Then, she remembered him telling her to call him if she needed anything, so she figured *"Why not?"* Reaching into her purse, she pulled out his number and after a brief pause, she picked up the phone and dialed his number.

***

Just as he was leaving his office, Wesley heard his phone ring and momentarily considered not answering it. Then, against his better judgement, he did and was glad when he heard Eyvette's voice.

"Good morning, may I speak to Brad Wesley, please?"

"This is Mr. Wesley speaking."

"This is Eyvette Summers."

"Oh hi, Ms. Summers, how may I help you?"

"Well, actually I'm calling because there's something I need to talk to you about and it's very important."

"That's fine," Wesley replied, "and I hope I can be helpful."

"Well, I'd rather not discuss it over the phone and I was hoping that we could maybe meet for lunch?"

"That won't be a problem because I'm actually free for lunch, but if you don't mind me asking what it's about?"

"I need to talk to you about the conversation we had concerning the younger generation."

"Are we talking about the younger generation in general, Ms. Summers?"

"Well to be honest with you, I need to talk to you about my son. I mean, I know we've just recently met, but I don't know who else to call."

"Oh, it's not a problem," Wesley replied. "In fact, I'm glad you called and I'll be happy to help you anyway that I can."

"Thank you, Mr. Wesley, I really do appreciate it."

"Don't mention it. So where would you like to meet?"

"There's a little café on seventeenth avenue and sixteenth street."

"Oh yeah, I know exactly where it is, and their Cuban sandwiches are delicious."

"So, you've been there?"

"Been there? I know the owner." Wesley replied.

"For someone who works at a brokerage firm, you sure do get around."

"Let's just say I had a life before I got this job."

"Seems to have been quite an interesting one."

"Yeah, well what time do you normally take your lunch break?"

"Around twelve, but I'm considering taking an earlier one today, say eleven?"

"That's fine and shall I order you one of those famous Cuban sandwiches?"

"Yeah, though I don't normally eat them. I guess I'll see you then."

"Ok," Wesley replied, "and I look forward to seeing you."

Hanging up the phone, he paused for a minute as he thought about what could be so important that she would call and ask him to meet her for lunch. She'd mentioned something about her son, but could it be that she just wanted to see him? He hoped so, because after dealing with what he had to deal with that morning, seeing her would definitely be a welcomed change.

***

"There, I did it," Eyvette thought to herself as she sat staring at the files on her desk. Now the question was, how would she explain to him that her son stashed a bag full of drugs in her house? And how would he react? It's been a while since she'd confided in anyone, but what made this situation even more difficult was that it involved her son. She hoped she'd made the right decision and only time will tell. Meanwhile, she had a job to do. Grabbing her casefiles, she left her office and headed for the courtroom.

CHAPTER 21

"Hey, anybody seen Clarence?" Spoon asked as he met up with Germ, James, and Rick by the stairs.

"Nah," Germ replied. "And when I called his house, ain't nobody answered."

"See, this the shit I'm talkin' 'bout. We out here tryin' to get some money and he off somewhere bullshittin'."

"Well one monkey don't stop the show," James replied. "Me and Rick can handle his shit till he gets here, 'cause we ain't got time to be waiting 'round for nobody."

"I feel you," Spoon said.

"Yeah," Germ added. "Me and you can handle this end while Rick and James cover the other side."

"That'll work, and when y'all need some more work, just come holla at me."

"Sounds like a plan to me, and we might as well get started 'cause a nigga tryin' to get some money, feel me?"

"Yeah, I feel you," Spoon shot back. "Anyway, y'all wait right here 'cause I'm gon' give y'all three ounces to start with and when Clarence do show up, we'll see 'bout getting the work y'all got cooked and bagged."

"Alright, go ahead and get that so we can get started," and as Spoon left to go get the work, Germ, James, and Rick waited by the stairs.

"Man, that nigga Spoon seems like he's straight," Rick said.

"Yeah, he is," Germ replied. "But what made you say that?"

"Nah, I'm just checkin' out how he handles his business. Plus, he don't mind letting other niggas eat."

"Most niggas be wanting to be greedy, but not Spoon. He feels like it's the young niggas' time to get some money, and he's tryin' to put as many of 'em on as possible."

"What's up with y'all homeboy Clarence?"

"Man, I don't know what's up with that nigga. We've made almost two thousand and five hundred dollars apiece in two days and if you ask me, that ain't bad."

"Hell, nah!" James screamed. "If we get both sides jumping like that, we'll keep this bitch open twenty four seven."

"Damn right," Rick said as they all looked up to see Spoon approaching, and suddenly stopping in front of them, he handed James three ounces. Then turning to face Rick, he pulled out a pistol and handed it to him.

"What's up?" Rick asked in surprise.

"Just a little something in case niggas wanna act crazy. Remember, we're kind of new round here, so keep it just in case."

"Oh don't worry, if a nigga come looking for trouble, he coming to the right place."

"That's what I'm talkin' 'bout. Oh, and if Clarence is 'bout the bullshit, we ain't fuckin' with him no more, you feel me?"

"Yeah, I feel you," Germ replied. "But man, I don't know what's up with him."

"Me neither, but we'll see when he gets his ass here. Till then, we got business to tend to so let's handle that."

***

Arriving early, Wesley parked his car and got out before going inside and taking a seat in the back of the café.

"Hood!" He heard someone scream and as he looked up, he spotted his old friend Demarco headed his way.

"Hey Demarco, how's it going?" He asked while standing to greet him.

"Long time no see! What brings you by here?"

"I'm meeting a friend for lunch."

"Let me guess, a woman?"

"You can say that."

"Still a lady's man, huh?"

"Yeah well, Demarco listen, this lady friend doesn't know me as Hood so I'd appreciate it if you wouldn't call me that in her presence."

"Oh ok, no problem," Demarco replied. "So what shall I call you?"

"Just Wesley will be fine."

"Must be some woman friend with you being so formal."

"It's a little more complicated than that, but I don't have time to explain right now."

"No need to, my friend, you want me to call you Wesley, I'll call you Wesley. Now what's been going on with you?"

"Same as always, trying to make a living."

"Yeah right, I hear you're this big executive now."

"Well, I can't run the street all my life."

"I guess you've got a point, but you mean to tell me that you're not in the business anymore?"

"I wouldn't exactly say that, but why do you ask?"

"Because like you, I'm not exactly out of the business either."

"Good, 'cause I just might look you up."

"You do that my friend, and I give you good deal like before."

"I'll keep that in mind, but here comes my date, so we'll talk later."

"Most definitely. In the meantime, what are you having?"

"Bring me two of your famous Cuban sandwiches and two sodas."

"Coming right up," Demarco said, "and your lady friend is beautiful."

"Go on," Wesley replied smiling, then turning to Eyvette he stood before pulling out her chair. "Good morning Ms. Summers, you look lovely today."

"Yeah, well I look better than I feel," she replied while taking a seat. "Oh, and good morning to you."

"Bad day, huh?"

"Bad night is more like it. I didn't get any sleep."

"Sounds bad."

"You don't know the half of it."

"Well now that we're here, why don't you tell me about it?"

"That's just it, I don't know where to start or if I should even be telling you this. I mean, you hardly even know me and here I am telling you my problems."

"Ms. Summers, I understand that you're this tough prosecutor and all, but you're still human and sometimes we all need someone to talk to."

"Yeah I know, but this is different."

"Why, because it involves your son?"

"That has a lot to do with it, but mainly because I'm usually the one in control and right now, I feel so helpless."

"Well I'm not gonna pressure you to talk to me, but just know that I'm here to listen and offer advice if you need me. Plus, whatever we discuss will remain between us."

"Thanks Mr. Wesley, but do you mind if I ask a question?"

"No, not at all."

"Ok then, what makes a young man or anyone else for that matter decide that they want to become a drug dealer?"

"Whoa! Where did that come from?"

"Just answer the question, please?"

"Well, it could be a number of things."

"Would you care to elaborate?"

"Well for one, most people generally sell drugs to make money."

"What if he has it already, or shall I say, his family does?"

"Then he could be doing it to obtain material possessions or to seem tough to his friends. Then, there's the female angle."

"Which is?"

"Well you see, Ms. Summers, most of the decisions men make involve two things. One is to make money to gain status among his peers and the other is to attract the opposite sex."

"How does a man think that by selling drugs he'll attract women, Mr. Wesley?"

"Easy, 'cause by selling drugs he can buy the material possessions that attract women."

"Some women," Eyvette replied. "Because some of us are smart enough to make our own."

"I agree, but not all women think like you, Ms. Summers. You see, while most smart women want their own, there are quite a few who do not and a man with money, fancy cars, jewelry, and nice clothes can be quite appealing. Then, you have to consider the excitement he brings versus someone who's routine is to go to work and then home every day."

"Going to jail and having to look over your shoulder every moment of the day wouldn't be my idea of excitement."

"That may be true, but you can't speak for all women 'cause what may not be exciting to you could very well be to them."

"Yeah well, I wouldn't want a man who didn't consider himself good enough to do anything other than sell drugs, and I definitely wouldn't want to be up at all times of the night worrying about if something's gonna happen to him."

"Again, that's your opinion."

"Well, women who are attracted to men like that need to raise their standards, because as long as they're accepting these men in their lives, they're not gonna want to do better."

"I agree with you one hundred percent," Wesley replied. "Now I have a question for you."

"Ok, what do you want to know?"

"What makes you so concerned about why men choose to sell drugs?"

"Well..." and before she could answer, Demarco had returned with their food.

"Ah here we are, two Cuban sandwiches and two sodas. Now can I get you anything else?"

"No, that will be all for now," Wesley replied. "Unless the young lady wants to order something?"

"No, this will be fine, thank you."

"Well if you change your mind let me know, ok?"

"Ok," Wesley said before watching Demarco leave. Then looking across the table at Eyvette, he said, "Enjoy your food. You can answer the question later."

As the two of them ate in silence, Eyvette thought to herself, *"How am I gonna answer his question?"* then decided the best way is to just tell him the truth.

CHAPTER 22

"Man, where the fuck you been?" Spoon screamed as Clarence walked up.

"I overslept." Clarence replied.

"You overslept! Nigga, we've been out here since seven a damn clock tryin' to get this money. And you mean to tell me that you couldn't get your ass out of bed earlier?"

"Spoon listen, I ain't got time to be going through this bullshit with you, alright? I got enough problems with my ole woman breathing down my neck. I overslept, what's the big deal?"

"What's the big deal!" Spoon screamed. "Well I'll tell you. For one, you're supposed to be handling the spot on the other side of the apartments, but instead you want to lay your ass in the bed for half a fuckin' day. Then you come 'round here talkin' about you ain't got time to be going through shit with me. Nigga, you the one ain't handling your business, but you know what? It's alright, 'cause James and Rick are doing just fine."

"Damn nigga, we homeboys. How you gon' let some niggas you just met run my shit?"

"Your shit? Nigga, let me tell you something. This my shit and I run it how I want to run it. Me and Germ the ones who went in the house and got the work and we brought your ass in, now you talkin' 'bout 'your shit.'"

"Damn right," Clarence shot back. "We agreed that I would handle the other side of the apartments while you ran this side."

"Yeah, but for some reason, you seem to think that you can come 'round when you get ready. You over there in your big ass house with your mama giving you everything, so you act like this is a game. But it ain't, 'cause some of us gotta grind for ours and if we don't beat our feet, we don't eat."

"What that gotta do with anything?"

"A lot, 'cause if you ain't gon' take this shit serious, you ain't got no business out here."

"Oh, so it's like that?"

"Damn right it's like that, and you know what else?"

"What?" Clarence replied.

"A nigga don't give a fuck if you don't come 'round here no more."

"So you gon' switch out on a nigga like that?"

"Damn right, and you know why? 'Cause you one of them niggas who wanna get paid, but you don't wanna put in no work. Well, you got a nigga fucked up."

"Nah I ain't got you fucked up, I got you figured out. You done got that shit and made a little money, now you got the big head. It's all good though, 'cause I don't give a fuck. If you'll let that shit come between us, I don't need to be fucked up with you anyway."

"Good, 'cause I don't give a fuck either," Spoon replied. "Oh, and another thing. I'll be by your house later on to get my shit."

"I'll save you the trip nigga, 'cause it ain't there."

"What the fuck you mean it ain't there? That's where it better be."

"My ole woman found it last night and flushed it down the toilet, so ain't no need for you to bring your ass round there."

"Nigga, I know damn well you ain't just say that your ole woman flushed my shit down the toilet."

"Well, that's what happened and ain't nothing I can do about it."

Suddenly without warning, Spoon grabbed the pistol from his waist, pointed it at Clarence and said, "Nigga, you're responsible for my shit, so either you or your ole woman owe me nine grand and I want my money."

"Man, hold up!" Germ screamed.

"Fuck this nigga," Spoon replied. "He think he gone come 'round here talkin' shit, then gon' stand here and tell me his mama flushed my shit down the toilet like it's alright."

"Yeah, but you ain't gotta shoot him! I mean, all of us growed up together."

"So what? It don't matter to him, so why should it matter to me?" Spoon said, then turning his attention back to Clarence who stood frozen in fear, he stepped closer to him. "Now like I said, either you or your ole woman owe me nine grand and I don't give a fuck where y'all get it from. You got till this weekend to get me all my money, or the next time I see you, it ain't gon' be no talkin'. Now get you bitch ass from 'round here."

As Clarence took off running, Germ looked at Spoon in disbelief. "Damn man, you gon' shoot Clarence?"

"Damn right, if he don't get that money up."

"But—"

"But nothin' nigga, and if you don't like it, you can go with him. See, you gotta show niggas that you ain't the one to be fucked with 'cause the first time they sense weakness, it's over."

"Yeah, but man, that's Clarence you talkin' bout."

"I don't give a fuck who it is, a nigga get out of line, he gon' get checked. Now we gon' stand here talkin' 'bout that nothin' ass nigga, or we gon' get some money?"

"Man, you said what you said, so let's get some money," Germ replied, and as they got back to handling their business, they had no idea that they were being watched by none other than Old Man Harry.

***

Back at the little café, Wesley and Eyvette were finishing up their lunch and as they pushed back from the table and relaxed, she looked up at him and smiled.

"Now, what was the question you asked me?"

"Oh yeah, I asked you what makes you so concerned about why men choose to sell drugs?"

"I asked because…"

"Hold up!" Wesley said, cutting her off. "If you don't want to discuss it, I'll understand."

"No, I need to get it off my chest 'cause if I don't do it now, I don't know if I ever will. Now, the reason I asked is because I think my son may be selling drugs."

"Whoa! Are you serious?"

"I'm afraid so."

"But what makes you think that?"

"Well, remember the other night when we had dinner?"

"Yeah, what about it?"

"Well when I left you, I went home, but when I got inside I smelled a funny odor so I began opening the windows to air it out. When I went into my son's room to open his window, I noticed a green duffel bag in his closet. But what made me notice it was the fact that I buy almost all of his things and I don't remember buying that for him."

"Wait a minute!" Wesley said, his mind now on full alert. "Did you say a green duffel bag?"

"Yeah, why?"

"Oh, just want to make sure I'm hearing you, that's all."

"Ok, I see the bag in the closet and like I said, I know I didn't buy it, so I pulled it out of the closet. Then when I opened it and saw the drugs, I couldn't believe it."

"How did you know it was drugs?"

"Mr. Wesley, I'm a prosecutor and I deal with drug offenses almost daily, so I know drugs when I see it."

"Oh yeah, I forgot about that. But you also know that kids nowadays are experimenting more than when we were growing up."

"I'm aware of that, but trust me, what's in the bag is too much for somebody to be just experimenting with."

"Well, how much is it?"

"I don't know, but it's quite a bit."

"Did you ask your son what he was doing with it or where he got it from?"

"I did, and he had the nerve to tell me that he was holding it for a friend of his."

"Some friends, huh?"

"Yeah, but I think he's lying because I also found fifteen hundred dollars that he had in his shoe."

"What did you do with the drugs?"

"I told him that I flushed it down the toilet."

"Ouch! I bet that didn't sit well with him."

"No, but I don't care 'cause he had no business bringing it in my house regardless of who it belongs to."

"I agree with you," Wesley replied. "But what do you want from me?"

"First of all, what do you think I should do with the drugs?"

"I thought you said you flushed it?"

"That's what I told my son, but between me and you, I still have it in the trunk of my car."

"Hold up! You mean to tell me that you're riding around with a bag full of drugs in the trunk of your car?"

"Well, I couldn't leave it at the house, and I'm definitely not giving it back to him."

"No, I not saying that, it's just…"

"Just what?" Eyvette asked.

"You shouldn't be driving around with it, that's all."

"That's why I'm telling you, 'cause I don't have a clue as to what to do with it."

"Ok, our first order of business is to get rid of it. Then, we'll figure out what to do about your son."

"Ok, but we'll have to get it out of my car."

"That won't be a problem, but there's one other thing."

"What?" she asked puzzled.

"You said you found fifteen hundred dollars he had hidden, right?"

"Right."

"Did you put that in the bag, too?"

"Yes, why?"

"Because I need to know what you want to do with it."

"I don't care, I just don't want it in my house."

"Why? I mean, it's not like you sold drugs to get it."

"So? I know where it came from and that's a good enough reason for me."

"Alright then, how about I donate it to one of the girls and boys clubs?"

"That's fine, I'm sure they can use it."

"Ok, then let me pay the tab and I'll be ready to go. It should only take a minute."

As Wesley went to pay for their lunch, Eyvette thought about how helpful he'd been even though he didn't have to be. He'd listened to her problems, offered her advice, and now he was willing to get rid of a bag full of drugs to help her son. Watching him return, she wondered what it would be like to… But she never finished her thought.

"Come on," he said before walking off and after following him outside, they approached her car.

While looking around nervously, she unlocked the trunk before reaching inside for the bag. Then after removing it, she handed it to Wesley who quickly walked to his car, unlocked it, and placed the bag on the backseat. "You alright?" he asked after walking back over to her.

"Yeah, but what are you gonna do with it?"

"Don't worry, I'll get rid of it. Now the question is, what are you gonna do about your son?"

"I haven't figured it out yet."

"Well think about it and once I've gotten rid of this stuff, we'll talk about it."

"Ok, but be careful."

"Oh, trust me, I will," Wesley replied and as he turned to walk off, she stopped him.

"Thank you, I really do appreciate what you're doing."

"It's not a problem. I mean, I did tell you that I'd do what I could to help, didn't I?"

"Yes, you did."

"Well, now you know that I'm a man of my word. Now I've gotta go get rid of this stuff, but I'll call you later on."

"Ok and again, thank you." She replied while watching him walk to his car.

Finally reaching it, he climbed in and grabbed the bag from the backseat. After placing it on the seat next to him, he opened it and immediately recognized the packaging. Realizing that it was some of the missing work, he silently wondered about the rest of it. Then after removing the fifteen hundred dollars from the bag and putting it in his pocket, he closed the bag, put the car in gear, and headed to Moose's house.

CHAPTER 23

"Hey girl, what's up?" Sheila said while greeting Carla at the door.

"I just came by to return the tapes I borrowed from you."

"Girl, get your butt in here and tell me how things are going with you."

"You wouldn't believe some of the things I've been doing," Carla replied while stepping inside of her friend's apartment and as Sheila closed and locked the door behind her, she took a seat on the couch.

"Well if you followed my advice, I can imagine," Sheila said while sitting next to her.

"I've tried most of it, but I don't know if I can do the anal thing. That looks like it hurts."

"Don't knock it till you try it, but I understand. It ain't for everybody. Now enough of that, I want all the details."

"Dang, you nosey."

"Well, you wanted to learn how to be a freak in the sheets and I want to know how my student is doing."

"Oh alright, but the first time you laugh at me, I'm leaving."

"Girl please, I love dick just as much as the next woman so why would I laugh at you for getting yours? Shit, who knows, you might teach me a thing or two."

"Oh I don't know about that, you're way more experienced than me."

"Carla listen, just because I date different men doesn't mean I sleep with all of them. For instance, my friend Larry can lick my pussy until I pass out, but he ain't got nothing but a two-inch dick. Now Boston, he'll fuck me till I can't walk, but he don't have a clue when it comes to eating pussy."

"What about that other guy?"

"Who, Alex?"

"Yeah, him."

"Oh all he wants to do is spend money on me and show me off to all his friends. He ain't never seen me naked."

"Are you serious?"

"Girl, you gotta lot to learn about men."

"I guess I do, huh?"

"Hell yeah, but don't worry 'cause when I'm through with you, that man of yours will be wrapped around your finger."

"You think?"

"Trust me, I know. How you think I got all this? And not one cent of my money goes to any of it."

"Alright then, I guess I've got a good teacher, huh?"

"Damn right, now tell me what you've done so far and I want all the details."

"Ok, the thing with the dildo worked out fine because now I can take him all the way in without gagging."

"Ooh! And I bet he loves that."

"Yeah, he can't get enough. Oh yeah, and I swallowed for the first time last night."

"You go girl. Damn, you learn fast."

"I wanted to see what it was like."

"Well, what do you think?"

"Tasted kind of salty, but it was alright."

"Don't worry, you'll get used to it. Have him drink more pineapple juice, it'll give it a sweeter taste."

"Ok, I'll remember that."

"Now what else?"

"Well, we've tried every position you can think of, and there's this one position where I lay on my side while he holds one of my legs in the air. It feels like he be all up in my chest."

"Yeah, that's called the scissor position and girl, you get nothing but straight dick."

"Tell me about it, but I do like it when he gets it from the back."

"Ohh! That's doggystyle, one of my favorites." Sheila said excitedly. "Shit! Just thinking about it make me want some."

"Girl, you so crazy."

"I'm serious, I mean, what's better than being with someone you care about and both of you are happy?"

"You got a point."

"Damn right, and remember this. What you won't do for you man, another woman will."

"Oh, you ain't gotta worry," Carla replied. "'Cause I plan to keep him happy."

"Good, now tell me more."

"Well, ain't really much else to tell you. I mean, I'm learning, but I want to do something he'll never suspect."

"Like what?"

"I don't know, but I want it to be something that'll blow his mind."

"Shit! Unless you fuck him into a coma, I don't know what else you can do."

"Well, let me ask you a question. Have you ever fantasized about doing a threesome?"

"Are you serious?"

"Well, I notice on the tapes you gave me when two woman were together, they just seemed like they know how to please each other."

"I've noticed that too, but a woman would know how to please another woman because we know what we like and how we like it."

"Well, have you ever fantasized about doing it?"

"Yeah, but that's not something you just do with anybody. Let me ask what you think, would you feel comfortable watching another woman sleep with your man?"

"It depends."

"On what?"

"Whether I trusted her or not."

"Now, who do you know that you can trust like that?"

"I'd trust you," Carla replied while turning to face her friend.

"Hold up now! I mean, we're best friends and all, but this is some deep shit."

"I know, but who else could I trust? All the things that I'm learning to do, he can go out and find another woman who'd do the same things, probably better. I want to do something that no woman has ever done before. Plus, I think it'll be exciting."

"Have you thought about what he's going to say?"

"He's a man, and what man you know would turn down the chance to sleep with two women at the same time?"

"Well, you do have a point. But Carla, that's your man."

"Yeah I know, but I want him to know how special he is and how much I love him."

"Why me, of all people?" Sheila asked.

"Because I trust you, and you're my best friend. On top of that, I wouldn't have to worry about anybody else finding out about it."

"You got that right," Sheila replied while suddenly standing and pacing back and forth. "Ok, just say we do it, then what?"

"I don't know, what you mean?"

"What I mean is, do we forget it ever happened, do we continue doing it, or what?"

"I don't know, what do you think?"

"Well honestly I wouldn't want to interfere with yours and his relationship."

"I don't think it'll do that," Carla replied. "Bit it will add a little excitement to our relationship. Plus, we'd have satisfied our curiosity."

"Ok I tell you what, think about it some more and if we decide to do it, you can't tell nobody."

"Alright, but you definitely won't have to worry about that."

"Good. Now I got some food in the oven, you want a plate?"

"Nah, I'm gon' go home and wait for Wesley to get there, then we'll probably go out for something."

"Ok, but do you want to take another tape home with you?"

"Nah I'm good, but I'll call you and let you know what my decision is about the other thing."

"Alright, and girl, don't worry," Sheila said. "If we do it, we're gonna blow his mind for real."

***

Back at Moose's house, he'd just gotten off the phone with Old Man Harry who told him about how James and Rick were now hanging with the boys under the stairs. He also told him about the altercation between two of the boys which resulted in one of them pulling a gun on him. He also told him how they'd expanded their little operation to the other side of the apartments.

While sitting there trying to figure out what all of it meant, he decided to give Wesley a call and tell him.

"Hey, this Wesley, what's up?"

"Just taking a few pans out of the oven, but I got a call from Old Man Harry not too long ago."

"What he want?"

"Remember I asked him to keep his eye on those young niggas who hang out by the stairs?"

"Yeah, what's up with 'em?"

"Apparently, two of 'em got into some kind of altercation and one of 'em pulled a gun on the other one."

"So they're beefin' 'bout money already, huh?" Wesley replied.

"Man, ain't not tellin' with these young niggas nowadays."

"Yeah you're right, but the one who pulled the gun violated the number one rule in the streets."

"Which is?" Moose asked.

"Never pull a gun if you don't intend to use it."

"I know that's right, but that ain't all. Remember those two niggas that were tryin' to sell the work?"

"Yeah, what about 'em?"

"They're hanging with the ones from under the stairs."

"Say what!" Wesley screamed.

"Those two young niggas we took to Old Man Harry's apartment are now hanging with the young niggas from under the stairs."

"What the fuck!"

"Yeah, and not only are they selling dope under the stairs, but they've branched out to the other side of the apartments."

"Yeah, and I think I know where they got the dope." Wesley replied.

"Where?"

"From out your house."

"Wait a minute! How you figure that?"

"'Cause the other two had two keys, remember?"

"Yeah I remember, but those young niggas from under the stairs were already there when we took the other two to Old Man Harry's apartment."

"You know what, you're dead right. So that means they already had our dope," Wesley said. "Plus, I found some of it today."

"Hold up! Man, what the fuck you talkin' bout?"

"It's a long story, but I'm on my way to your house now and I'll explain it to you when I get there."

"Alright, but hurry up 'cause I want to hear this."

"Yeah, you just be easy till I get there." Wesley replied before hanging up.

CHAPTER 24

"Oh so what, you're a cowboy now?" Sonya screamed as soon as Spoon walked through the door.

"Damn, what the fuck you talkin' 'bout now?" Spoon replied.

"Boy don't play, why you out there pulling guns on people?"

"How you know about that?"

"You must have forgotten where you at. Everybody 'round here stays in everybody's business. People blowing up my phone telling me that you out there pulling guns on people."

"That's what's wrong with ma'fuckas now, always in another ma'fuckas business," Spoon replied angrily.

"Well, I'm listening," Sonya said as she stood with her hand on her hips.

"Listening for what?"

"I want to know why you pulled a gun on the boy."

"'Cause he playin' with my money, that's why."

"Who was it, Spoon?"

"What difference does it make?"

"You forgot I got a daughter who lives here and I don't need nobody shootin' up my shit because they looking for your ass."

"Well, you ain't gotta worry 'bout that, 'cause Clarence ain't gon' shoot nobody."

"Clarence!" Sonya screamed. "Ain't he supposed to be your friend?"

"Fuck him."

"Oh, so you gon' let a little money come between you and your friend?"

"If you call nine thousand dollars a little bit of money, hell yeah."

"How did Clarence come to owe you that much money?"

"I gave him some shit to hold for me and he had it stashed at his mom's house, but he claims she found it and flushed it down the toilet."

"Well, I can see why you'd be mad at him, but you still didn't have to pull a gun on him. What if you would've shot him?"

"Then he'd be one shot ma'fucka."

"Boy, that's still your friend and y'all shouldn't be falling out over no money."

"Yeah I hear you, but he better have my money the next time I see him."

"Or what? Spoon, let me tell you something. They had a nigga name Todd who used to sell dope 'round here and he started doing the same shit."

"What same shit?"

"Pulling guns on people and disrespecting them for no reason. You know what happened to him?"

"Nah, what?"

"They started calling the police and the feds came and got his ass."

"So what's that got to do with me?"

"I'm just telling you, 'cause if you start that crazy shit, they gon' do the same thing to you, and I don't want to see that happen."

"Look Sonya, as long as a ma'fucka respect my shit, they won't have a problem," Spoon replied.

"That's what's wrong with you niggas now, y'all sell a little dope somewhere and y'all think y'all own shit. These apartments been here before you came around and they gon' be here when you're gone."

"Yeah, but right now I got shit on lock, so a ma'fucka better recognize."

"You know what," Sonya said in disgust, "do what you do, 'cause I see you gon' have to learn the hard way."

"Oh you talkin' that shit now, but I'm gon' see if you go be talkin' like that once you see all the money a nigga gon' be making."

"Money ain't everything," Sonya screamed. "What good it's gon' do if you're dead or in jail?"

"Man, I ain't tryin' to hear all that," Spoon replied, then grabbed some work from the bag and headed for the door.

As he reached the door, Sonya yelled, "Spoon!"

"What?"

"Don't be out there with the bullshit."

"Yeah yeah, I hear you," he said before stepping outside and closing the door behind him.

***

Pulling up in front of Moose's house, Wesley parked his car, reached over, and grabbed the bag before climbing out. Walking up to the front door, he looked to his left and noticed Moose's neighbor watering her yard while watching him. After knocking a couple of times, Moose opened the door and greeted him.

"Damn, what took you so long?"

"Are you gonna at least let me in before you interrogate me?" Wesley asked.

"Oh yeah, come on in," Moose replied while eyeing the duffel bag Wesley was carrying.

"Hey man, your next door neighbor was looking at me like she wanted to kill me or something."

"Oh, that's just Ms. Marshall," Moose said smiling. "Ever since those ma'fuckers broke in here, she watches everybody like a hawk."

"Yeah, well, you need to let her know that I'm family."

"Alright, I got you. Now what's this about you got some of the work back?"

"Here's a quarter key of it right there," Wesley said while holding up the bag.

"Where did that come from?"

"There's a lady I met and she found it in her son's bedroom closet."

"Did she ask him where he got it?"

"She said she did, and he told her that he was holding it for a friend of his."

"You think he's telling the truth?"

"Who cares, what I want to know is who is this so called 'friend.'"

"Yeah I feel you," Moose replied.

"You want to know what I think?"

"What?"

"I think he's friends with the ma'fuckas in the apartments."

"What makes you say that?"

"Think about it. If you had somebody holding something for you and he told you that his mom flushed it, how would you react?"

"I'd be pissed."

"Would you be pissed enough to pull a gun on him?"

"It depends."

"On what?"

"Whether I believed him or not."

"Ok, but didn't Old Man Harry call you and tell you about the altercation between two of those young niggas in the apartments?"

"Yeah, but you think that was the reason?"

"Maybe it is. I mean, it fits, doesn't it?"

"Well yeah," Moose replied. "But how do we find out for sure?"

"Honestly, I'm thinking 'bout asking him myself."

"Man, you can't be serious."

"Moose, I'm always serious when it comes to my shit."

"Yeah, but it's gonna seem kind of strange you asking 'bout four and a half keys, don't you think?"

"I'll have a little more tact than that, but you see, his mom knows me as Wesley and to her, I'm just a concerned citizen tryin' to help."

"Now that's funny," Moose replied. "But how do you plan to find out where the rest of our shit is?"

"Well, the plan is for me and her to sit down with her son to find out why he decided to try and sell dope in the first place."

"Shit! To get some money, what else?"

"Nah, this is different, 'cause he's not one of those kids who has to. I mean, his mom has good job and makes good money. Plus, he's an only child, so he's basically spoiled."

"So in other words, what you're saying is that he's doing it to look cool or he's doing it because pressure from his friends?"

"That's exactly what I'm thinking," Wesley replied. "And if that's the case, his friends under the stairs got the rest of our shit."

"Who is this woman with the good job? Anybody I know?"

"Her name is Eyvette Summers, but I don't know if you know her.

"Where does she work?"

"At the State Attorney's Office."

"At the State Attorney's Office!" Moose screamed. "What does she do?"

"She's an Assistant Prosecutor."

"Oh shit! You mean to tell me that this lady friend of yours is a prosecutor in the State Attorney's Office?"

"That's right."

"And her son had a quarter key of cocaine in his closet?"

"Right again."

"Then on top of that, instead of turning him in, she calls you and you playing the upstanding citizen role agreed to help by getting rid of it for her?"

"That's about right, and that's how I found out that it's some of the dope that was stolen from you house."

"Now I've heard some crazy shit in my life, but this has got to be the craziest."

"Why?"

"Man, she's a prosecutor."

"So? She's also a mother whose son is in trouble and I'm the Good Samaritan that's helping her out. Now how hard is that?"

"Man I don't know, I mean, what if she suspects something? You know how those people's minds work."

"What she gon' do, lock me up? Then she'll be getting herself and her son in hot water. Her for not reporting a crime and him for having the dope in the first place."

"Yeah I hear you, but still…"

"What?"

"She's still a prosecutor."

"Yeah, but who knows, it might be to our advantage."

"How?"

"We might need her help someday, so it's a good connection to have."

"Alright, well just be careful."

"Don't worry, all I'm tryin' to do is get our stuff back, or at least find out who got it."

"I can feel that, but you're cutting it kind of close, don't you think?"

"Hey, I like living on the edge," Wesley replied smiling. "Oh yeah, which reminds me, I told Ms. Summers that I'd call to check on her after I got rid of the bag, so I'm gon' get out of here."

"Alright and like I said, be careful."

"Yeah, no doubt.

Leaving his friend's house, Wesley got in his car, started it up, put it in gear, and headed home, but not before calling Eyvette.

CHAPTER 25

Clarence was still shaken up by the fact that Spoon had pulled a gun on him. Pacing back and forth in his room, he thought about what Spoon had said about having the money by the weekend and realized that there was no way he'd have it by then. He also remembered what Spoon had implied if he didn't have it. He wondered if he would really shoot him. Anger swelled up in him as he recalled his mother saying, "I flushed it down the toilet," and figured it was her fault that he was in the predicament he was in.

Suddenly, he heard his mother's car pulling into the driveway and sliding the gun under his pillow, he walked into the living room just as she was coming through the door.

"Have you been here all day?" She asked.

"Yes, ma'am," he lied.

"You didn't have anybody in my house, did you?"

"No."

"Good, now sit down, 'cause we need to talk."

"Ah ma, haven't you done enough already?"

"Boy, sit down like I told you before I go up side your head."

As Clarence did as he was told, his mother took a seat across from him.

"Now you want to tell me why you want to run the streets and sell drugs like you ain't got no sense?"

"I told you, I wasn't selling drugs," Clarence replied. "I was just holding it for a friend of mine."

"Alright, since you want to stick with that story, who is this friend who got you stashing drugs in my house?"

"Why you want to know all that?"

"'Cause I want to know who's got you doing what you're doing."

"Ain't nobody got me doing nothing, and I told you it won't happen again."

"Well, it shouldn't have happened in the first place. Why didn't he stash it at his own mother's house? Oh I know, because he got your stupid behind to bring it here, that's why." Eyvette said sarcastically.

"Ma, didn't we talk about this last night?"

"Boy do you realize how much trouble you could've gotten into if you would've gotten caught with that stuff?"

"But I wasn't gonna get caught with it."

"Oh, so you're some kind of super criminal now."

"No."

"So what is it, you think you're too smart to get caught? 'Cause sooner or later, if you keep doing what you're doing, you're gonna get caught and I won't be able to do nothing to help you."

"Ma I'm eighteen, I don't need a babysitter anymore."

"Clarence, let me tell you something. Turning eighteen doesn't make you grown and until you're able to take care of yourself, it's my responsibility. Now, I don't know what you want to do with your life, but all running the streets is gonna get you is either dead or in jail. You may still be mad at me for flushing your friend's or whoever the stuff belonged to down the toilet, but I did it for your own good."

"My own good!" Clarence screamed, "Do you realize that because of what you did, I might not even have any more friends? Plus, what am I gonna do when he comes looking for his stuff?"

"First of all, anyone who would convince you to stash drugs in your mother's house ain't your friend, especially if he ain't stashing it in his own. Second, tell me his name and I'll tell him that I flushed his stuff down the toilet."

"What difference is that gonna make? He's still gonna want his money, and you tell me where I'm gonna get nine thousand dollars to pay him."

"Clarence, you are my son and your wellbeing is all I care about. Now if someone comes bothering you about that stuff, let me know and I'll get the authorities involved."

"You just don't get it, do you?" Clarence asked.

"Get what?" Eyvette replied.

"If you call the police, everybody will call me a snitch. Then my life will really be ruined."

"Clarence, I don't care what people think, all I care about is that nothing happens to you."

"Well I care, ma," Clarence replied. "And I'll deal with it however I gotta deal with it."

"And what's that supposed to mean?"

"It means just what I said. Out in the streets, you don't call the police to deal with your problems, you handle them yourself."

"Clarence! You wasn't raised in the streets, so I don't know where that mentality comes from, but let me tell you something, you're my only son and I'm not gonna lose you to the streets. You might want to be stubborn and that's alright, but remember that I can be stubborn, too. Now after tonight, I won't say another word about it. But you try me if you want to mister, and I'll show you better, that I can tell you." She said sternly, and without another word she stood and walked out before closing the door behind her.

While getting undressed, she thought about the challenges of raising a young black male in today's society and knew that as a parent, she must take a more active role in her child's life if he was gonna make it. She'd drawn the line in the sand and given him something to think about, but if he wanted to test her, let him. Because he was going find out just how determined she really was.

***

Walking into his apartment, Wesley smelled the sweet aroma of food cooking, and it suddenly hit him that he hadn't eaten since lunch. He smiled as Carla came out of the kitchen to greet him. "Hey handsome, dinner will be ready in about twenty minutes."

"Good, 'cause I'm starving," Wesley replied. "What are we having?"

"Well, we have rice, corn, Jiffy Cornbread, and I fried some chicken."

"Damn! What's the occasion?"

"You being here with me," she said while eyeing him seductively. "Now go take a bath and get ready for dinner. I've already run your bath water and your clothes are sitting on the toilet."

"How 'bout you come wash my back?" he asked playfully.

"I've got to finish cooking dinner, but trust me, there will be enough time for that and other things once we eat."

"Ohh! Now I like the sound of that."

"Good, now go on before the food burns," Carla replied and while watching him head towards the bathroom, she thought about how much she loved him.

From the first day they'd met, she didn't have to work and he'd given her everything her heart desired. Several minutes later, Wesley came out of the bathroom wearing the silk boxers that Carla had laid out for him, and while entering the kitchen, he noticed that she'd changed into a red see-through negligée. Instantly becoming aroused, he began caressing her breasts.

"What are you doing?" She asked smiling.

"What does it look like?" he replied while continuing to caress her gently.

"Well it looks like you're about to let the food get cold if you keep doing that."

"How can you expect me to concentrate when you're wearing this?"

"It's part of the allure, Wesley."

"The what?"

"Sort of like temptation, boy."

"Well, I'm definitely tempted."

"Just relax, we're trying something different."

"How is this trying something different when you're walking around naked?"

"That's just it," Carla replied. "You can look, but don't touch. In the meantime, the anticipation grows and when we do touch each other, we both will be ready to explode."

"Shit! I'm ready to explode now."

"Yeah, I can see," Carla said while looking at his hard-on. "But trust me, I'm worth the wait. Now come on, let's eat."

Wesley stood watching her ass jiggle as she walked off, and he didn't know how long he'd be able to look at her without touching.

Carla smiled to herself as she gazed back at his hard-on, and while serving him his food, she deliberately brushed up against him. She'd promised to make it worth his while, and she was definitely going to keep her word.

Seated across the table from each other, Carla sat with her legs open, giving him a bird's eye view of her neatly trimmed pussy. He knew exactly what she was doing, and smiled to himself because it was working. Although he'd love to throw her down on the table and fuck her brains out, he knew that she was making an effort to keep their sex life exciting. During the meal, he stole glances at her and fantasized about the things he wanted to do to her. Then he had an idea. Finishing up his food, he smiled at her from across the table, then as she stood to remove his plate, he grabbed her, lifted her up, and set her on the edge of the table.

"Wesley!" she screamed.

"Shhh!" he replied while pushing her legs a part, and suddenly relaxing, Carla looked on as he began licking the inside of her thighs. Sliding her negligée to the side, Wesley pushed her legs back farther, and after kissing a trail up her leg, he ran his tongue up and down between the folds of her pussy. Closing her eyes and biting her bottom lip, Carla squirmed as he flicked his tongue back and forth across her clitoris and suddenly increasing his pace, it didn't take long for an earth shattering orgasm to tear through her body. After lapping at her juices, he looked up at her and smiled.

"Damn! That was good."

"Yeah well you're not the only one who wants desert," she replied while climbing down off the table.

While he looked on, she removed his boxers and kneeled down in front of him. Then after running her thumb across the head of his dick, she took him in her mouth. He moaned with pleasure as her head bobbed up and down in his lap, and minutes later he came flooding into her mouth with his juices. After licking him clean, she stood and kissed him passionately, then reaching for his hand, she pulled him up and led him to their bedroom.

CHAPTER 26

Business was good in the apartments, and to show everybody just how good, Spoon and the rest of them decided to treat themselves. Spoon bought a 2009 Chevy Avalanche, painted it a Jolly Rancher Candy Green, and had it sitting on a set of 30-inch three-piece Ballerz Inc. Luxury rims with two-inch Toyo Tires. James traded in his Grand Prix and copped an all-black 2010 Cadillac Escalade EXT on 28.7-inch Lexani CS-2s and Toyo Proxy tires. Not to be outdone, Rick bought a candy-painted 71 Donk, complete with a chromed out nose sitting on color matching 24-inch Dub Remixes, and rounding out the group, Germ got himself a 75 Caprice Convertible, painted it pearl white, and fitted it with a set of 26-inch Lexani rims and Toyo Tires.

Pulling into the parking lot of the apartments, they all parked and got out when Germ spotted Old Man Harry walking to his old and rusty pickup.

"Hey, ain't that the old man who's always watching us?"

"Yeah," Rick replied. "But man, fuck him."

"Damn right," Spoon said. "That old ma'fucka just better respect our shit."

"Damn! Who's that?" James suddenly asked.

"I don't know, but she's finer than a ma'fucka."

"Hell yeah, and I'm goin' to holla at her," James said before walking off.

Walking up to the apartments, all eyes were on them, and they loved the attention. Even Germ had a few admirers, but he didn't have the confidence to talk to any of the girls. That was all right, because Spoon had enough for both of them and he let it be known as he walked with his head held high. Finally reaching Sonya's apartment, Spoon opened the door to find her sitting on the couch watching TV and as soon as he closed the door, she turned to face him.

"Spoon, I need to talk to you," she said before heading for the bedroom.

"Damn!" Spoon replied while turning to Rick and Germ. "Y'all just chill while I go see what she wants."

"Yeah, alright," Germ said as they watched him go in the room.

"Yeah, what's up?" he said after closing the door behind him.

"Why you went and spent all that money on that damn truck?"

"Man, what the fuck you talkin' 'bout? All I did was buy a truck."

"Spoon, I ain't stupid."

"And I never said you was."

"So why you spent all that money on a truck when we're living in a damn two bedroom apartment?"

"Girl, why you trippin'?"

"Ain't no 'why I'm trippin',' 'cause you're acting just like the rest of them niggas out there. Time y'all get a little money, y'all start acting stupid."

"Damn Sonya, you trippin' like this 'cause I bought a truck?"

"It ain't 'bout the truck, Spoon, it's about the attention you're bringing on yourself. Not to mention, you got your priorities all messed up."

"How you figure that?"

"'Cause for one, we're living in a two bedroom apartment, and instead of trying to invest the money you're making in a house, a business, or something, you go out and spend it on a truck, paint, and rims. Oh yeah, and another thing, you've been around here for about a month, haven't you noticed that the police ain't been around here yet?"

"Yeah, but that's only because my shit's air tight," Spoon replied.

"Nigga please, they ain't been around here 'cause they ain't had no reason to suspect that anything was going on. Now what you think go be on their minds when they ride through here and see all them pretty cars out there? How you gon' explain living 'round here, but yet you can afford a truck like that?"

"It ain't their business where my money comes from."

"You know, I thought you were smarter than that, but I see now I gave you too much credit."

"What the fuck you mean by that?"

"What I mean is, in case you didn't know, selling drugs is illegal and the last thing you want to do is bring attention to yourself."

"Oh, so you my mama now?"

"Nah, I ain't your damn mama."

"Well that's what you sound like."

"Why, 'cause I'm telling you what's right?"

"Nah, 'cause you tryin' to tell me how to run my shit. What you want me to do, ride around in a raggedy ass car?"

"Spoon listen, I ain't got no problem with you buying a car to use for transportation, but it don't have to be that fancy ass truck. Don't you realize that that's why so many niggas end up broke? And if something happens, they end up having to go to trial with a public defender."

"Well I'm the one out here busting my ass to get this money," Spoon replied. "And I feel like I'm entitled to buy myself something nice to show for it."

"Ok, so why didn't you use the money you spent on that truck as a down payment on a house? Oh, so now you can't talk, huh? Well let me tell you something, I don't plan to grow old living in this damn apartment. I want better for myself and my daughter and everything I do is for that purpose because I feel I deserve better. Now you and me have agreed to do this relationship thing, but I'm not gonna put up with you out there running the streets acting like you ain't got no sense. That might be alright for them other niggas, but they ain't my concern, you are. So you need to start handling your business."

"Alright, I listened to you, now you listen to me. You want to talk shit 'bout me spending money to buy me a truck, but I don't hear you saying nothing when I give you money to go shopping, or to get your hair and nails done."

"Spoon, all you give me is fifty dollars a week to get my hair and nails done. You spent damn near forty thousand dollars on that truck. And for your information, the money you give me to go shopping, whatever I don't spend on bills and to put food in the refrigerator goes in the bank. If you don't believe me, here's the five hundred dollars you gave me the other day," she screamed as she reached into her dresser drawer and showed it to him. "Y'all niggas go out there and spend y'all money on bullshit, then when it's all gone, y'all sit around talkin' about 'I had this' or 'I had that.'"

"Well I ain't like them other niggas, plus I ain't going to jail 'cause my shit's tight."

"Nigga, please! But like I said, you're hard headed, so you gon' have to learn the hard way."

"Yeah, well, I ain't got time to stand here arguing with you 'bout it 'cause I got money to make."

"Yeah, you go right ahead, 'cause all you want to do is run the streets with your friends anyway, but if your ass go to jail, don't call me."

"Man, I ain't trying to hear all that," Spoon replied, "I'm out of here."

Walking into the living room, he said to Rick and Germ, "Man, y'all come on, 'cause a nigga ain't tryin' to be arguing with her right now."

"What's wrong with her?" Germ asked as they stepped outside.

"She trippin', that's what," Spoon replied as James suddenly met back up with them and appeared excited.

"Hey man, you know the girl I went to holla at?"

"Yeah, what's up with her?"

"She says her name's Sabrina, and she asked me to give her a ride home."

"Damn! Where she live at?"

"In the apartments on one eighty thrid street and forty seventh avenue."

"That's right up the street."

"Yeah, and she says she got a couple of friends, so y'all want to follow me or what?"

"Hell yeah," Rick replied, "I just hope they look like her."

"I don't know 'bout all that, but she went to go get her stuff from her aunt's house and she'll be back in a minute."

"Alright, we gon' wait on y'all, then we'll swing by there to see what's up."

Minutes later, Sabrina came back and her and James got into his truck before pulling off with the others right behind them.

***

Pulling up in front of Moose's house, Old Man Harry parked his truck, got out, and walked to the door. He was about to knock when it suddenly opened.

"Hey old timer," Moose said smiling.

"Yeah it's me, but how'd you know I was out here?"

"My neighbor called and told me."

"Damn! What is she, the president of the crime watch association?"

"You can call it that, 'cause ever since somebody broke into my house, nothing or no one gets past her."

"So what does her old man say about what she's doing?"

"Nothing 'cause she doesn't have one, she's a widow."

"Well in that case, I might go knock on her door."

"Get your ass in here and tell me what's on your mind."

"Well actually, I'm thinking I ought to go next door and give that old gal something to do besides peak out the window all damn day."

"What you gon' do old man, talk her to sleep?"

"I reckon she'll be asleep after I'm done with her, but it won't be because we was talking, if you know what I mean."

"You leave my neighbor alone, you hear me?"

"Yeah I hear you," Harry replied. "But come to think of it, she might put me to sleep. You know my energy ain't what it used to be."

"Yeah, tell me about it," Moose said laughing. "So what's up?"

"Well, you know them young boys you asked me to keep an eye on?"

"Yeah, what about 'em?"

"Well, whatever they're doing, they're starting to make some good money."

"What makes you say that?"

"For one, all them pretty cars and trucks they're buying. You know the ones with the fancy paint jobs and those big rims?"

"Yeah I know what you're talking 'bout, so you say they're buying cars and trucks, huh?"

"Yeah, got the parking lot looking like a crayon box."

"Well you know, Wesley was by here last night."

"What did he want?"

"He believes those same boys are the ones who stole our dope."

"Man, you bullshittin'!" Harry screamed.

"Nah, but he wants to be sure before we go over there and confront 'em."

"How will he ever be sure unless we catch 'em with it?"

"Oh, so you haven't heard yet?"

"Heard what?"

"That Wesley found some of the stuff?"

"Hold up! What you mean he found some of the stuff?"

"Well this lady friend of his—"

"A woman had our shit!" the old man screamed.

"No, a woman didn't have it, but if you'd shut up and listen, you'll understand what I'm trying to tell you."

"Oh alright, go ahead."

"Like I was saying, this lady friend of his found it in her son's bedroom closet still in the bag they took from the house. Now she doesn't know anything, but apparently she told her son that she flushed it down the toilet."

"But she didn't?"

"No, she gave it to Wesley to get rid of."

"So let me get this straight," Old Man Harry said. "This lady, a friend of Wesley's, found our stuff?"

"Some of it." Moose replied.

"Ok, some of it, in her son's room closet and she told him she flushed it, but that was a lie because she gave it to Wesley to get rid of?"

"Right so far."

"How much was it?"

"A quarter key."

"So somebody still got the other four and a quarter keys?"

"Right again."

"So what makes Wesley think the youngsters from the apartments got something to do with it?"

"Well, he believes that this lady's son and the boys from the apartments were friends."

"What you mean 'were'?"

"You remember you called and told me how you saw one of 'em pull a gun on the other one?"

"Yeah, and he thinks it's because the one boy had to tell his friend that his mama flushed the shit down the toilet?"

"Yeah, that about right," Moose replied.

"Son of a bitch!" Harry screamed. "So that's probably why every time I look around, one 'em watching me."

"What are you talking 'bout?"

"There's this one, I think they call him Germ or something like that. Anyway, he always seem to be watching me."

"You think maybe they know who we are?"

"Most likely," Harry replied. "But the thing is, they don't know if we know that they're the little ma'fuckas who broke in your house and stole out shit."

"Well let's keep it like that till Wesley can find out for sure," Moose said.

"Shit! I say we bum rush the sons of bitches and get our shit back," Harry screamed.

"Hold our horses Old Man, if we knew for sure that's one thing, but we don't so till we do, we have to play it cool."

"Yeah I hear you," Harry replied, "I don't like it, but you're right. I tell you what though, if it turns out that they got our shit, Lord have mercy on 'em."

"I'm with you on that Old Man, but in the meantime, just keep an eye on 'em."

"Oh, I'm gonna do that regardless and the first time they get out of line, I'll be there to catch 'em."

"Yeah, you just call us and we'll come give you a hand."

"Man I don't need no help with them youngins. I mean, I can whop all four of them at the same time."

"I believe you, Harry," Moose replied, "But just promise me that you'll call before you do anything."

"But I can."

"Promise me, Harry."

"Oh alright, I promise."

"Promise what?"

"That I'll call before I do anything. There, you satisfied?"

"Yeah Old Man, I'm satisfied."

"So when's Wesley supposed to find out this information?"

"Hopefully soon."

"Well I hope so, 'cause I'm itching for a scratch, you know it's been a while since I had a good one. Matter of fact,

I'm going home to clean my guns 'cause I want to be ready when the shooting starts."

"Well hopefully it won't come to that," Moose replied.

"Shit, that's all this generation know how to do and they can't even do that right. They end up killing everybody except the people they shootin' at."

"Yeah, you got that right Old Man. But anyway, go on home and remember to call us if you hear or see anything."

"Alright, but you let me know as soon as Wesley finds out anything."

"Will do," Moose replied before watching Old Man climb up into his truck and drive off. As Harry drove off, a thought hit him. What would happen if one of those youngsters pulled a gun on him, or even shot him? Could he kill someone who was young enough to be his grandchild? It didn't take long for the answer to come to him, and he smiled as he answered his own question, *"You damn right!"*

CHAPTER 27

Exhausted from their night of love making, Carla laid in bed as Wesley showered, got dressed, and prepared to leave. The night before, as he brought her to countless orgasms, she'd thought about the conversation she'd had with Sheila concerning the threesome and was convinced that it would be the perfect surprise. Then again, it was something she wanted to experience for herself as well.

Watching him walk back and forth gathering his things, she climbed out of bed and made her way over to him before hugging him.

"You want me to fix you something to eat before you leave?"

"Nah, that's ok. I'll pick something up later."

"Well has your boss called to tell you when it would be ok for you to come back to work?"

"No, but I'm gonna call him to see what's going on. Now what are you getting into today?"

"Sheila's throwing a surprise party for one of her boyfriends and she asked me to help her with the decorations."

"That sounds like it'll be fun, but how's she doing?"

"Oh, she's alright."

"I haven't seen her in a while, but tell her I said hi."

"I will, you just make sure you call me later."

"Yeah ok, now let me get out of here 'cause if I don't leave now, I never will," he replied while squeezing her ass.

She watched as he grabbed his car keys and headed out the door. After hearing the elevator door open and close, she picked up the phone and dialed Sheila's number. After several rings, she heard her friend answer, "Hello!"

"Yeah, this is Carla."

"Oh hey girl, what's up?"

"Just thought I'd call to see what you was up to."

"Girl, I ain't doing nothing but washing some clothes, that's all. And I'll probably do a little cleaning."

"Well, have you thought about what I asked you the other day?"

"Yeah, but have you decided what you really what to do?"

"Well, kind of."

"What does that mean?"

"Well honestly I want to do it, but I don't want you to feel uncomfortable."

"Carla I'm a big girl, and there isn't much that makes me uncomfortable."

"Ok, then since you put it like that, I want to do it."

"Alright, now that that's out of the way, the next question is, how do we make it happen?"

"Well I was thinking that maybe while we're doing it, you just come in the room and join in."

"Nah, that sounds too tacky, besides, we wouldn't want to make him nervous."

"Ok, how 'bout this. I get him in the shower and when we come out and go the bedroom, you're already in bed waiting."

"You know," Sheila said, "let me think on it and I'm sure I'll be able to come up with something. In the meantime, nobody can know about this and Carla, I mean nobody."

"Oh, don't worry," Carla replied. "And thank you for agreeing to do this."

"No problem, I mean, what are friends for?"

"Well that's why I came to you, and I'm sure he's gonna enjoy it."

"Yeah," Sheila said, "I just hope it doesn't backfire."

"Anyway, I won't hold you up any longer. Just give me a call later.

"Ok I'll do that, and don't worry about a thing."

"Well thanks again," Carla said before hanging up and setting the phone down, she sat for a moment thinking, *"Ok Mr. Wesley, I truly hope you're ready for this, 'cause it's definitely gon' be a night to remember."*

***

After pulling into the parking lot of the apartments on 183rd Street and 47th Avenue, James and Sabrina sat in the truck talking when Spoon got out and walked over to the driver's side window.

"What's up?" James said while rolling down the window.

"Man, I thought you said she had some friends over here."

"Damn nigga, chill, she's going to get 'em now." James replied, and while they both looked on, Sabrina got out of the truck and walked into the complex.

"Damn! I hope her friends look like her." Germ said.

"I know, that's right," Spoon said. "'Cause baby girl's finer than a ma'fucka."

"Yeah, but you know girls like that usually hang out with ugly broads," Germ said laughing.

"I tell you what, if her friends are ugly, I'm out of here." Spoon replied.

"Yeah, me too," Rick joined in.

"Well, y'all can take y'alls pick," James said as they all looked up to see Sabrina returning with three of her friends.

"Damn, lil' mama's thick," Spoon screamed.

"Which one?" Germ asked.

"The one with the blue shorts."

"Well I got the one with the jeans on," Rick said.

"Y'all can have 'em 'cause I like the other one," Gem added, and as the girls walked up, Spoon spoke first. "How y'all doing?"

"Oh, we alright," the girls said in unison.

"Oh yeah, so what's your name?"

"Jasmine."

"And how old are you, Jasmine?"

"Old enough."

"Old enough, huh?"

"Yeah, now you've asked us questions," Jasmine replied. "But what's your name?"

"Everybody call me Spoon, but check this out, let's me and you walk over here and talk for a minute."

"Alright, come on," she said, and as the two of them walked off, Germ and Rick began talking to the other girls.

Now standing by this truck, Spoon looked Jasmine up and down and liked what he saw.

"So tell me a little something about yourself."

"Ain't much to tell really. I live here with my mama and brother. I don't have any kids and I work at the stadium."

"What stadium?"

"Sunlife Stadium."

"What you do over there?"

"I work at the concession stand, but I'm trying to get into nursing school."

"So you live here with your mama and brother, huh?"

"Yeah."

"How old is your brother?"

"Nineteen, why?"

"Oh, I was just asking."

"What, you're looking for somebody to work for you or something?"

"Nah, why you say that?"

"Sabrina told us y'all the niggas who got the apartments on fire, so I figured you was tryin' to get somebody to work for you over here."

"You know, that might not be a bad idea," Spoon replied. "Your brother know anything 'bout running a spot?"

"Him and his friends were doing a little something around here, but the nigga who they were getting their stuff from is a buster."

"Why you say that?"

"'Cause he was running around talking all that boss shit, and come to find out he was working for somebody else."

"Yeah I feel you, but you ain't gotta worry 'bout that with me. If I decided to open up shop over here, I might holla at your brother, but right now I'm tryin' to holla at you."

"What you tryin' to holla at me about?"

"About me and you getting to know each other better."

"First of all, where's your girl?"

"Where's your man?"

"I don't have one 'cause I ain't got time for the bullshit," Jasmine replied with an attitude.

"What bullshit?"

"You know how y'all niggas get, especially when y'all get a little money."

"Well, I ain't with all that," Spoon said. "All I'm looking for is a ride or die chick, somebody who's gonna be down for me and me only."

"How you know I'm not one?"

"I don't, but I'm willing to find out if you are."

"I'll have to see, 'cause y'all niggas get a female all in her feelings then y'all go to acting all crazy."

"Well I'm like this, if you're straight with me, I'm gon' be straight with you. But if you gon' be with the bullshit, I'll go find somebody else."

"I tell you what, give me your number and I'll call you and we'll talk about it."

"Alright," Spoon replied before reaching into his truck for something to write his number on and after writing it down, he handed it to her. "Now don't take my number if you ain't gon' call."

"Oh I'm gon' call, I just hope no hoes call my phone talking about you their man."

"You ain't gotta worry 'bout that 'cause like I told you, as long as you straight with me, I'm gon' be straight with you."

"Alright then, we'll see."

"Yeah we will," Spoon said. "And tell your brother I might wanna holla at him."

"Alright, I'll tell him," Jasmine shot back before turning to walk off.

"Damn! A nigga can't get a hug before you go?" he suddenly asked.

"First of all, we just met," she replied while turning back to face him. "But if you're all what you say you are, you'll get more than a hug, so chill and I'll call you."

"Alright then," Spoon said smiling as he stood watching her walk off, and once she'd disappeared inside the complex, he walked over to where Germ and Rick stood talking to the other girls.

"Man, what's up, y'all ready to go?"

"In a minute," Rick replied, "but Monique here wants to go get a little something to eat later on."

"Yeah, Crystal here do, too," Germ said. "You going?"

"I don't know yet, but Jasmine gon' call me later so I'll see what's up. In the meantime, I'm gon' head back over to the apartments, so y'all holla at me when y'all leave here."

"Alright, we got you," Rick shot back.

"Where's James?"

"Him and that girl Sabrina sittin' in his truck talking."

"Well, tell him to come by the apartments when he gets through, 'cause we still got money to make."

Without waiting for a reply, Spoon turned and began walking to his truck when a strange feeling came over him. Ignoring it, he climbed into his truck and after starting it up, he looked up to see someone watching him from one of the apartment windows. Thinking that Jasmine was getting her peak on, he smiled to himself before putting his truck in gear and driving out of the parking lot.

CHAPTER 28

Wesley wanted the rest of his dope, and that was the bottom line. Driving down Biscayne Boulevard, he thought about Eyvette and her son, and wondered how he could get the information without seeming anxious. Then after careful thought, he decided the best approach was the direct approach. Pulling out his cellphone, he dialed Eyvette's number and after several rings, she answered.   "Hello?"

"Yes, Ms. Summers, please."

"This is she, but who's calling?"

"This is Wesley."

"Oh hey, good morning, Mr. Wesley."

"Good morning to you, too," Wesley replied, "I hope I'm not disturbing you."

"Oh no, not at all. Matter of fact, I decided to take the day off, so I'm kind of just lounging around the house."

"I guess everybody needs a break sometime, huh?"

"You are so right Mr. Wesley, an in my line of work, it's a much needed one. I see that you're out and about today, what's goin' on with you?"

"Well like you, I decided to take a couple of days off. You know, to relax a bit.

"I can understand that."

"Yeah, but I was calling to see how things were going with you and your son?"

"He's still mad at me, but I don't care. One day, he'll realize that it was for his own good."

"We hope so, but I was wondering, well not wondering, but actually hoping that we could get together sometime. You know, the three of us, because I'd love the chance to talk to him and maybe find out what's going on in that head of his and hopefully be able to help other kids like him."

"You know what, that's a wonderful idea. I mean, with his father being absent from his life, having a strong male figure to talk to would probably do him some good."

"That's only if he'll talk to me."

"Oh he'll talk, trust me."

"How can you be so sure?"

"Because I'll go upside his head if he doesn't."

"I see somebody's gotten on your bad side."

"Well, kind of. You see, I used to give him more freedom, but after that stunt he pulled, it's something he has to earn back."

"That's a good point because I think that's one of the things the younger generation is lacking. We as adults don't take the time to teach them responsibility. Now mind you, all of us want them to have the things we didn't growing up, so we tend to try to make up for that by giving them everything but in all actuality, we're raising a generation of kids who feel like the world owes them something."

"Well, this one's gonna learn that what you get out of life is what you earn. I mean, it may seem that the easy way is the best way, but looking at the state of our communities, there's nothing easy about going to jail."

"You're absolutely right, and that's why I'd like to take the two of you to lunch. At least it'll give me an opportunity to meet him, and hopefully I can get him to understand the dangers of making bad decisions."

"Well somebody needs to, 'cause I can't seem to make him understand it."

"You're not alone, Ms. Summers, 'cause with the incarceration rate being what it is for our young black men, many women are left to raise young boys. Now while many are doing a fine job, it's just hard for a woman to teach a boy how to be a man."

"I agree Mr. Wesley, plus this luncheon will give us both the opportunity to get out of the house."

"Ok, then how about y'all meet me at the Chinese restaurant on one eighty third street and sixty seventh avenue?"

"The one in the plaza by American Senior High?"

"Yeah, so I see you're familiar with the area."

"Familiar with it?" Eyvette replied. "It's my favorite place to eat."

"Oh, really?" Wesley said, "Well what do you know, it's my favorite, too."

"Good, so what time would you like for us to meet you?"

"How does one o'clock sound?"

"Perfect."

"Well, one o'clock it is then."

"Don't worry, me and my son will be there."

"Fine, so I'll see you then."

"Ok, bye."

Hanging up the phone, Wesley looked at his watch and saw that it was only eleven thirty, so he decided to go see Moose before meeting Eyvette and her son. Besides, it was about time to collect the money from his last shipment.

***

After hanging up the phone with Wesley, Eyvette walked down the hallway to her son's room and knocked.

"Yeah?!" Clarence screamed from inside.

"Boy, don't you 'yeah' me, open the door," she quickly replied, and hearing the door unlock, she opened it and stepped inside. "What are you doing in here?"

"Nothing but playing video games."

"Well, you need to cut that off and clean up your room."

"Ah man, my room's clean already."

"You call this clean?" Eyvette asked while glancing around the room. "Anyway, I'm tired of you being stuck up in this room, so I'm taking you to lunch."

"What if I don't want to go?"

"I'm not asking you Clarence, besides, there's somebody I want you to meet."

"Who, another one of your boyfriends?"

"Boy, don't make me hit you in the mouth. He's not my boyfriend, but he's a good friend of mine and maybe he can talk some sense into that head of yours."

"Well he'll be wasting his time, because ain't nothing to talk about."

"Oh no? So I guess you think stashing drugs in your mama's house is normal, huh?"

"You're still talking about that?"

"Yeah I'm still talking about it, and I'm gon' keep talking about it until you realize that that isn't the type of life you want to live."

"Well you flushed it down the toilet so we ain't gotta worry about that, now do we?"

"Look Clarence," Eyvette said moving closer to him, "I understand you're still mad at me, but I did it for your own good."

"My own good!" Clarence screamed, "Ma do you realize what you've done? If I don't have the money for that stuff by this weekend, Spoon is gonna—"

"Gonna what?" Eyvette suddenly asked, cutting him off.

"Nothing, 'cause you wouldn't understand."

"How can I understand when you won't talk to me?"

"Ma, that stuff you flushed cost nine thousand dollars and because of what you did, I have to figure out a way to pay him by this weekend."

"Or what, Clarence? Has he or anybody else threatened you? 'Cause if he has, I'll call the authorities."

"Don't you get it, ma? I can't call the police."

"Why not?"

"Because everybody will call me a snitch, then I really couldn't show my face."

"Well, I stand by my decision to flush it because I can live with you being mad at me. What I couldn't live with is if something happens to you. Now if this Spoon person, whoever he is, tries to harm you in any way, I'll have him arrested and prosecuted to the fullest extent of the law."

"Ma, haven't you done enough already?" Clarence replied. "Now would you please let me handle it from here?"

"Handle it how, Clarence?"

"However I got to."

"Clarence, I'm not gonna just stand by and watch you throw your life away because you feel like you got to prove something to somebody. Now you listen to me, and you listen good. You are not gonna end up a statistic because I raised you better than that. Your so called friends might think it's cool to run the streets and throw their lives away, but you're not gonna do it, that I promise you. I'm not trying to win a popularity contest, and I don't have to be your friend, but I'm still your mother. So like I said, I'm taking you to lunch and I expect you to be ready to go by no later than twelve thirty, do you understand me?"

"Yes, ma'am."

"Good, now I have a few things I need to do before then, but you think long and hard about what I said."

As she headed for the door, she suddenly stopped and turned to face him and said, "Oh yeah, and clean up your room like I told you," before walking out and closing the door behind her.

About The Author

Marlin Ousley is an author and the founder of Circle Six Publishing. A Miami, Florida native, Marlin exhibits an uncanny ability to capture the pulse of the streets with intelligence, strong character development and well thought out storylines. He has a Bachelor's Degree in Business Management and an Associate's Degree in Public Relations. His first novel "Taking No Shorts," a first in a trilogy, has received critical acclaim from critics and readers from around the country. He has three children, Lil Marlin, Anthony and Alexandra, and he's hard at work on his next novel.

Other books by Marlin include "Ghetto Fabulous" and "Chasin Paper"

We Help You Self-Publish Your Book

You're The Publisher And We're Your Legs.
We Offer Editing For An Extra Fee, and Highly
Suggest It, If Waved, We Print What You Submit!

Crystell Publications is not your publisher, but we
will help you self-publish your own novel.

Don't have all your money? .... No Problem!
Ask About our Payment Plans
Crystal Perkins-Stell, MHR
Essence Magazine Bestseller
We Give You Books!
PO BOX 8044 / Edmond – OK 73083
www.crystalstell.com
(405) 414-3991

---

n 1-A   190 - 250 pgs $719.00   **Plan 1-B   150 -180 pgs $674.00**

Plan 1-C   70 - 145pgs $625.00

'ublisher/Printer) Proofs, Correspondence, 3 books, Manuscript Scan and Conversion,
eset, Masters, Custom Cover, ISBN, Promo in Mink, 2 issues of Mink Magazine,
sultation, POD uploads. 1 Week of E-blast to a reading population of over 5000 readers,
k clubs, and bookstores, The Authors Guide to Understanding The POD, and writing
s, and a review snippet along with a professional query letter will be sent to our top 4
ibutors in an attempt to have your book shelved in their bookstores or distributed to
ntial book vendors. After the query is sent, if interested in your book, distributors will
act you or your outside rep to discuss shipment of books, and fees.

an 2-A   190 - 250 pgs $645.00   **Plan 2-B   150 -180 pgs $600.00**

Plan 2-C   70 - 145pgs $550.00

rinter Proof, Correspondence, 3 books, Manuscript Scan and Conversion, Typeset,
ters, Custom Cover, ISBN, Promo in Mink, 1 issue of Mink Magazine, Consultation,
) upload.

We're Changing The Game.

No more paying Vanity Presses $8 to $10 per book!

Made in the USA
Middletown, DE
24 September 2021

48257919R00130